The Agony of the Ghost

THE LIBRARY OF BANGLADESH

HASAN AZIZUL HUQ

The Agony of the Ghost
and Other Stories

TRANSLATED BY BHASKAR CHATTOPADHYAY

CALCUTTA LONDON NEW YORK

Seagull Books, 2018

Original stories © Hasan Azizul Huq, 2015

Translation © Bhaskar Chattopadhyay, 2015

ISBN   978 0 8574 2 502 7

THE LIBRARY OF BANGLADESH series was conceived by
the Dhaka Translation Center at the University of Liberal Arts Bangladesh.
Find out more at http://dtc.ulab.edu.bd/

Printed in arrangement with Bengal Lights Books

This edition is not for sale in Bangladesh

British Library Cataloguing-in-Publication Data

A catalogue record for this book is available from the British Library

Typeset and designed by Sunandini Banerjee, Seagull Books, Calcutta, India,
using artwork from the Bengal Lights editions
by Narottama Dobey and W. Basher

Printed and bound by WordsWorth India, New Delhi, India

CONTENTS

LIBRARY OF BANGLADESH

An Introduction

The independence of Bangladesh, while into its fifth decade now, is still viewed by many outsiders as an accident of history. All historical outcomes are in part an accident, but any event of the magnitude of Bangladesh's liberation can only happen as a consequence of deep and long-term agency. What underlies that agency in this case most decisively is a unique cultural identity.

Like the soft deposits flowing down from the Himalayas that created the land mass known as Bangladesh today, its culture too has resulted from centuries of diverse overlay. Generations here have always gravitated towards the mystical branch of the reigning faith, be it Buddhism, Hinduism or Islam. The net effect is a culture that has always valued tolerance and detachment over harsh rituals or acquisitive fierceness.

There is no way better than Bangladesh's literature to know what makes this unique and vital culture as full as it is of glory and, of course, foibles. How did a rain-washed delta full of penniless peasants turn into a leader among developing nations? How did the soft, mystical, Baul-singing population turn into one of the fiercest guerilla armies of the last century? How did love of the Bangla language trigger the very march to freedom? How do the citizens of the world's most densely populated city, barring only a few tax or gambling enclaves, make sense of daily life, and find any beauty, amid all the breathless din of commerce and endless jostle of traffic?

The first three books in this series provide a remarkable window into the realities and mindscape of this amazing, confounding, rich world through translations of three of the living legends of Bangladeshi writing: Syed Shamsul Haq, Hasan Azizul Huq and Syed Manzoorul Islam. The presentation of their work has been made possible by the Dhaka Translation Center, hosted by the University of Liberal Arts Bangladesh. It also owes a great deal to the tireless efforts of its Director, Kaiser Haq. The series owes most, however, to award-winning translator Arunava Sinha, who both helped conceive of this idea, and helms it as series editor. Eminent translators brought together by him have ensured a rare and truly world-class rendition of these hidden gems of world literature. The impressive international-standard production owes everything to DTC's sister concern, Bengal Lights, led by editor Khademul Islam and managing editor, QP Alam.

Bangladesh, for all its success, is still to the world the sum of half-told stories told by others. It's high time to offer a fuller account of ourselves to the world. DTC plans to bring out at least three titles each year, and add both new names and new titles by selected authors to this defining series on Bangladeshi writing. We also believe that the process of consciously engaging new and wider audiences will lead to new refinements to a body of work that is already one of the great overlooked treasures of global writing.

KAZI ANIS AHMED
Publisher, Bengal Lights Books
Founder, Dhaka Translation Center

The Agony of the Ghost
and Other Stories

A
HELL
CALLED
HOSPITAL

The man at Emergency was busy looking at something on the table. He looked up absently and saw two middle-aged men and an old man carrying another man on their shoulders, standing a short distance away. The old man's thin long nose was crooked on one side. His short salt-and-pepper beard was dripping with sweat. The face of the man they were carrying was not visible; one of his legs was hanging in the air, while the other was hooked around the old man's shoulder. The rest of his body was curled around the shoulders of the two middle-aged men. The three men sighed heavily.

The man sitting on a chair in front of the emergency desk looked up, but he didn't seem to notice anything. The telephone rang. A knot appeared on the man's eyebrows. The telephone rang again. Another knot. When the phone rang for the third time, he hunched forward and picked up the receiver.

"Yes, Emergency."

He heard the voice at the other end and said, "I don't know."

Then after a few seconds, "No, I can't. There's no one here."

Putting the receiver back on the cradle, he bent over the desk once again, inspecting something minutely and plucking out short strands of hair from his nostrils with his unusually long fingers.

The phone rang once again. The man picked up the receiver once more.

"Yes, Emergency."

After sometime, he said, "Yes, so what? What are you going to do?" After listening to the caller for a few more seconds, "Yes, that's how it is. I can't send anyone now. There's no one here . . . Manners? Don't try to teach me manners. Who the hell do you think you are? Oh yes? Fine, do whatever you can. And don't ever call back."

He slammed the phone down, saying, "Complain, my ass!"

A warm breeze blew into the room through the open door and window towards the south. The two middle-aged men sighed heavily once again and switched the other man's legs from one shoulder to the other. The face of the man riding on their shoulders now came in full view. Dry, pale, bloodless. He licked his lips and looked around with those round eyes. The man at Emergency produced several knots on his eyebrows and asked, "What?" As he uttered this solitary word, his large ears turned crimson with rage.

The old man tried to adjust the position of the leg on his shoulder and said, "Huzoor!"

The phone rang once again. This time, the man snatched the receiver from the cradle and was just about to yell into the mouthpiece when suddenly his back straightened like an arrow, he jumped up to his feet, and rattled off in one breath:

"Yes sir, no sir, that's right sir, that's right sir, yes sir, all right sir, no sir, all right sir."

No sooner had he replaced the receiver on the cradle and wiped the sweat off his forehead than the phone rang again, startling him. He answered nervously, but a wide grin appeared on his face this time:

"Ah, it's you! How are you? No, no, I went there yesterday, yes yesterday . . . no hang on, the day before yesterday, yes the day before yesterday. No, no—in the afternoon. No, no . . . no one was there. That I don't know. No, they didn't make any arrangements . . . nah . . . nothing at all. Film? What film? Do you have any idea how busy I am? No, it was just bad luck yesterday, twenty rupees down the drain. Yes, don't I know that whore! Listen, I wanted to tell you, Dulu has come. Yes, you must have heard. Oh! You didn't know? Yes, his father . . . cancer . . . no, throat. Yes, hardly. No listen, listen, I won't be able to make it . . . no man, my wife will kill me. Yes . . . no, have fun . . . yes."

The man smiled once again and put the receiver down carefully. Then he looked up, wiped the smile off his face and said, "What is it?"

All three visitors looked weak and limp by now. The old man spoke up hoarsely, "This man is sick, huzoor!"

The man at Emergency snarled, "So, what the hell do you want me to do? Should I dance?"

"Where should we . . . ?"

"On my head!" Then he said in an irritated voice, "Put him down there. Put him on the floor."

The three men dropped the sick man on the floor in a hurry, as a farmer throws a yoke on the ground. The man fell on the floor with a thud. The leg hooked around the old man's neck made him collapse on the ground too, the knot of his lungi coming off, making him naked from the waist down. The old man looked up at the man at Emergency, who was once again concentrating on the surface of the table. Only he knew what treasure lay there. Meanwhile, the three farmers sat down on the floor, leaning against the wall. One of them unwrapped the gamchha from round his head and started fanning himself with it. The old man had managed to retie his lungi around his waist, this time with a double knot. "Huzoor!" he called out.

The man at Emergency looked away from them, at the distant wall.

One of the legs of the man carried in had swollen into a nasty mess. He spread out the leg, folded the other leg below himself and leaned against the wall, blinking. A steady stream of pus trickled down his swollen feet. A large blue fly circled around them for some time before alighting on them. Having surveyed the landscape and gathered all necessary information, it flew off to summon its kith and kin, who soon arrived in large numbers.

"What's the matter?" the man at Emergency asked again.

The old man repeated, "Huzoor!"

The other two continued to look around glumly.

"Where are you coming from?"

"Talpukur, huzoor!"

"What's wrong with his leg?"

"Huzoor, sir!" The man began. "He's dying, the pain . . . "

Four people burst into the room. The young man in front was brimming with excitement. Walking directly to the desk, he said, "Have you seen?"

The man at Emergency prised out a tiny speck of dirt from under his left thumb with his right one and said, "Seen what?"

"You haven't? Haven't you read the papers?" The young man perched on the desk, swinging his legs in the air like a child. The three men accompanying him all pulled up chairs and benches near the desk and settled down comfortably.

"They've announced the new pay scales, it's come out in this morning's papers. Haven't you seen?"

"Which paper? Dhaka?"

"No, the local paper. It's the same thing, this one's a national daily too."

"Nothing's going to actually happen," Emergency said. "The constipated government will take ages to shit those scales out, if at all there's any truth to it, which I highly doubt."

"One thousand takas!" the young man said. "Which grade will they put us in? Sixth or seventh, I wonder?"

One of the men sitting on the bench said, "Tell me, what use is it increasing salaries? Have you seen how prices are shooting up? Three hundred takas for half a quintal of rice. One hundred for the wife's sari. What's the use? How can they solve the bigger problem?"

Another man said, "Economics, my friend, economics! Screws our brains and fucks the hell out of us. It's not enough to raise salaries, bring down inflation too. In other words, increase productivity.".

The first man on the bench said, "Why even bother to pay us salaries?

Let the wife make a list of what she needs for the whole month, we'll take it and hand it over to the government. You are the government—you supply all this. I don't want your salary."

"Why else do you think the government is telling us again and again to increase productivity?"

The man on the bench suddenly burst out, "Shut up, you idiot. Increase productivity! I'll seal your asshole with mud and plant a crop in it. Increase productivity, my ass! Ask those farmers sitting over there about productivity. Well, Chacha, will you be able to increase productivity?"

The old man shifted uncomfortably and muttered hesitantly, "Huzoor, sir!"

The man on the bench laughed like a hyena, saying, "There! See? He's promised to increase productivity!"

The young man seemed somewhat crestfallen by now. He said, "In that case why did the government raise our salaries?"

Bench said, "I don't believe it—what the fuck is wrong with you?"

Emergency said, "It's a bluff. Has it come out in any of the Dhaka papers?"

The young man said, "That's not the point. The point is whether the government will raise our salaries."

The man who had not spoken a word so far now remarked, "It will."

"It will? Why?"

"Because the government wants to silence the educated class."

"As if the educated class ever speaks anyway! They have always kept their mouths shut, and I say it's better that way. We'll have to leave the country if they open their stinking mouths. Don't give me that educated class bullshit, I've seen enough educated class in my lifetime."

"Still, the government doesn't want to take any chances. It wants to keep them happy. After all they do make a lot of sense when they speak."

"Sense my ass! That's the kind of stupid thing you find in a democracy. What's the point keeping them happy in a military regime?"

Emergency said, "That's enough, get back to work now, all of you. This is the emergency desk! Stop yelling and gossiping."

The men walked away, still discussing and debating the issue. A blaze of heat seemed to enter the room riding on a warm gush of wind. The farmers were still sitting up against the wall. One of them had even begun to snooze. On the other side, beyond the open door, nurses in their starched spotless white uniforms were walking by with mincing steps.

"What's wrong with his leg?"

The old man started his story again, "Huzoor, sir!"

Emergency raised a hand and said, "What am I asking you? What's wrong with the leg?"

The old man made a valiant effort and said, "He went to the barber day before yesterday, and then . . . "

"The barber? Why?"

The old man rattled off, "Huzoor, sir, you could say about a month or so ago, yes one month ago, a thorn got into the sole of his foot. You could say around dawn, no, before dawn. He was going to shit in the field when a babul thorn, theeees big huzoor, sir—what, Zamiruddi? Did it bleed heavily that day, my boy?"

Emergency said, "How is he related to you?"

"Huzoor?"

"Are you his father?"

"No, huzoor, sir! I am . . . like an uncle . . . from the village. He . . . "

"And what about these two people?"

"They're no one, huzoor, not related. They are . . . just . . . like brothers."

"Why have you brought him here?"

"His father is dead, huzoor!"

"Fine, but why did you bring him here? Why didn't you dump him at home?"

The old man hesitated for a couple of seconds and said, "Because . . . the hospital . . . "

"Yes, the hospital. What about it?"

"Huzoor, where else can poor people like us go? The barber tried to open up the wound and pluck the thorn out the day before yesterday, and then all this started within a day. The pain is just too much, huzoor, sir, oh!" The old man groaned as though he were experiencing the pain himself. The other two farmers were still sitting up against the wall and looking around.

"There's nothing that can be done here," Emergency said casually and looked out at the blazing sunlight outside. After sometime, he said:

"Take him to Outdoor, get a ticket. Not today, everyone's left. Take him there tomorrow morning and get a ticket."

The old man didn't seem to understand. He simply stared blankly into the void. Zamiruddi tucked in his healthy leg and blinked rapidly.

Now Emergency rose to his feet. He was of a thin build, had strange webbed feet, and large spread-out ears. He must have been tall at some time in the past, but someone appeared to have twisted and bent his backbone halfway down its length. He stepped up to Zamiruddi and looked at the soles of his swollen feet. A thick stream of puss was flowing out of a wound. The blue flies were extremely busy. Squeezing Zamiruddi's toes, he asked, "Does it hurt?"

Zamiruddi nodded his head slowly to indicate that it did.

"Nothing we can do here." Emergency stood up and walked towards the door. As he got there, Zamiruddi silenced the noise in the hospital and the dry whistle of the wind with a deathly gasp. Emergency looked back over his shoulder and said once again, "Take him away, dump him at home, or take him to the graveyard. Go anywhere, but take him away from here." And then he walked out.

There was no one else in the room besides the four men. A high, narrow oilcloth-covered bench stood against the southern wall. Next to it a stretcher rested against the wall, looking like a ladder. The old man whispered, "What do we do now?"

One of the farmers yawned and said, "Does he want a bribe?"

The old man said, "Even if he does, who has the money? I've got just five annas."

"Then let's take him back. Zamiruddi, do you want to go back?"

Zamiruddi shook his head slowly to indicate that he didn't.

"What do we do then?" The old man was visibly worried.

In the meantime, two men rushed into the room, one of them young and the other middle-aged. The young man seemed very happy and excited, giggling and chattering constantly, "Come on, come on, grab it, grab the other end, oh fuck it!"

The middle-aged man was calm and composed. He said— "What's so funny, son of a bitch? You need to watch yourself, motherfucker!" The two of them picked up the stretcher and walked out of the room.

The old man looked at his two companions and said, "And now?"

The ceiling fan circling above their heads let out a dying rattle and resigned from its job. A tongue of fire snaked in from outside to lash the room. The two men came back with the stretcher. The strain of carrying a heavy load was evident on the middle-aged man's face. His eyes seemed to be popping out of their sockets. The young man's biceps had swollen. They held the stretcher at the same level as the oilcloth-covered bench and tilted it whereupon a man rolled out like a sack of sand and fell on the bench in a heap. With a flick of his wrist, the young man turned the stretcher on its end, set it against the wall, and dashed out of the room. The middle-aged man cursed in unprintable language and followed him.

The old man looked at the newcomer on the bench and realised that he was unconscious. His skull had cracked open at several places. His face was covered in blood, much of which had already clotted into a thick, hard, dark layer. A gaping wound just below one of his eyes was the only place from which red blood was still spurting.

"Oh God!" The old man covered his eyes.

One of the farmers had fallen asleep. Zamiruddi was still blinking incessantly.

"Where? Which way? Must be in here." A group of men walked into the room and gathered around the bench, examining the man lying on it.

"What was the number of the truck?" One of them said.

"I didn't get a chance . . . it drove away."

"Was there anyone in the rickshaw?"

"I don't know. It's crushed completely."

The Emergency man was now seen behind the group, with a doctor standing next to him. The doctor's white apron was impeccably spotless.

As soon as he pushed through the crowd, made his way to the bench and moved the unconscious man's head a little, a lump of pink-white brain matter oozed out of a hole in the patient's head and trickled down one of the legs of the bench.

In a cold voice, the doctor said, "Expired!" He stepped away from the bench.

"What is it? What's happened?" Several voices were heard.

"Is he dead?"

"Yes, he's dead."

The men in the group stared at the dead man's face for some time and walked out of the room without a word. After they left, the dead man's face came into view, his lifeless eyes fixed on the hot blue sky beyond the burnt blades of grass outside the door.

The doctor said, "And them?" The Emergency man shook his head.

The doctor stepped up to Zamiruddi and examined the wound with sharp eyes. After some time, he looked at the old man and said, "He won't survive. It's too late. There's nothing we can do anymore. How did this happen?"

The old man said calmly, "Huzoor, a month or so ago, he had stepped on a babul thorn. And then, just the other day, he had gone to the barber and . . . "

"That's enough, I get it. The barber did the rest. Take him away."

Zamiruddi had stopped blinking—his eyes had now filled with tears. Emergency stared at the floor. The doctor finally said, "Get his papers made and send him to the surgical ward. Not that they'll be able to help."

The doctor left. Emergency followed him out. The dead man's head lolled over the edge of the bench. The old man looked around, tiptoed quickly to the bench and placed the dead man's head back on it. Then he shut the eyelids of the corpse and sighed heavily.

Emergency walked into the room with the stretcher carried by the young man and the other middle-aged man. Pointing at Zamiruddi, he said, "Take him to the surgical ward."

The middle-aged man began to grumble. "We're humans too, you know? Isn't there anyone else around?"

Emergency patted him on the back and said softly, "Come on now, take him there. The poor thing wants to die in a hospital. Take him there!" He thrust a small piece of paper in the old man's hand.

With renewed vigor, Zamiruddi made a valiant attempt and dragged himself on to the stretcher by himself. The old man stepped into the inner corridor of the hospital. The two farmers hadn't moved an inch from their position, but both of them were awake now.

As the stretcher was being carried up a flight of stairs, it tilted so precariously that Zamiruddi almost slid off it. The young man managed to prevent him from falling off. When they entered a large room on the first floor, the two men tilted the stretcher to its side, dropping Zamiruddi on the floor with a thud, and literally ran out of the room. Zamiruddi made an effort to break his fall with his elbow, wincing in pain as he hit the floor and collapsed in a heap. Frightened by now, the old man walked up to a man sitting behind a table, who took the chit from his hand and asked, "Where's the patient?"

"There he is, huzoor." He gasped for breath.

"There're no beds. He'll have to remain on the floor. Will he be able to do it?"

"Sorry, what are you saying, huzoor?"

"I'm saying, there're no beds, can he remain on the floor?"

"Yes, huzoor, he will . . . ."

"All right, take him over there."

The old man looked in the direction the man had pointed out and saw several rows of iron beds. On the western side of the room, there was some space between two beds—barely three feet wide. Zamiruddi would have to be moved into this space. The old man held his head in despair. How on earth was he going to accomplish this mammoth task? Zamiruddi was lying at the doorstep, blocking the door. The old man walked up to him and said softly, "Zamiruddi, we're going to have to go over there, my boy."

Zamiruddi stared at him. The old man broke eye contact immediately, walking around and behind his body. He grabbed Zamiruddi by his armpits and tried to haul him along the floor through the labyrinth of iron beds. Despite Zamiruddi's best efforts to use his good leg to push himself along, the old man had to pause often, breathing so heavily that a shrill whistle seemed to ring out from his chest.

"Just a little farther, my boy," the old man said softly, wondering where to go, because by now his own vision had completely blurred. A countless number of patients seemed to be lying around, with others walking amidst them, talking. He heard nothing though, nor did he see anything. Having dragged Zamiruddi all the way to the specified spot as instructed, the old man collapsed against the wall. After gasping for several minutes, when he had managed to find his bearings, the man who had taken the chit from his hands walked up to the spot and said, "All right, good."

The old man wiped the sweat off his brows and said through shallow breaths, "What else do I need to do, huzoor?"

"Nothing, we'll do the rest."

"So, may I go then?"

"Yes you may."

The old man didn't know what else to say. The other man also didn't wait there any longer.

The old man said, "Zamiruddi, are you hungry?"

Zamiruddi let out a strange sound—a nasty, cold gurgle of sorts, like the cackle of a goose. It seemed to come from somewhere deep down within his throat, not from his tongue. The old man placed his ear near Zamiruddi's mouth and realised that although he was talking in a human language, he was quickly using up whatever little strength he had left in his body in trying to enunciate his words. It was impossible to decipher what he was saying without one's ear within an inch of his mouth.

"No." The single word tore through Zamiruddi's eyes and mouth as he struggled to pronounce it.

The old man rummaged through the pocket of his dirty old half-sleeved shirt and brought out a rock hard, sour and stale piece of bread. "Keep this, eat it when you're hungry."

Zamiruddi cackled again, "No."

"Keep it, don't say no."

Zamiruddi remained silent.

"I'll be on my way then, my boy?"

"Chacha!"

The old man once again placed his ear near Zamiruddi's mouth and said, "Tell me."

Exhaling his warm breath into the old man's hair, Zamiruddi said, "I'm going to die. We won't meet again. Don't mind anything I may have said."

The old man tried to protest. "Of course not. Why would you die?"

"You heard them, Chacha. Just do me a favour. Ask the doctors how long I have. If he says three or four days, see if you can bring the children."

"And your wife?"

"Yes, her too."

The old man stared at his face for some time and then looked for something at his waist. Then he said, "I know you don't have any money on you. Nor do I, my boy. Just these twelve annas, this is all I have. Keep it." He pried open Zamiruddi's huge fingers and thrust the coins into his sweaty palm. Zamiruddi clutched the old man's hand and squeezed it, and his eyes filled with tears.

The old man jerked his hand away roughly from Zamiruddi's and quickly walked out of the room without a backward glance.

The doctor walked into the room late in the evening with a group of other people behind him. His square face was covered with scars and pockmarks left by chicken-pox. His jaws were broad and strong. He strutted into the room and started walking between two rows of beds, throwing glances to his left and his right, and tossing off expert comments. "Isn't this that ulcer patient? He's still alive? That's odd. He's not supposed to have survived till now. But of course he will die, it's just a matter of a few more hours. I mean, if he survives the entire medical science will turn out to be a big lie."

He turned to his left next. "Gallbladder stone?" Then he winked at the apron-clad medical college students behind him and remarked, "Isn't he a police officer? Rich man! Gallbladder stone—heh! Hey, what the hell are you doing here?"

At once a dark, scrawny, little man sat up on his bed quickly and broke into an embarrassed grin behind his unkempt salt and pepper beard, like a cornered street dog.

The doctor growled at him, "How come you are still here? I want you out tomorrow. Listen, remind me to release this man tomorrow."

Having examined all the patients in less than seven minutes, the doctor then turned towards those who hadn't found a place on the beds and exploded. "Why are there so many patients on the floor?"

The man on duty came running, "We couldn't put them on the beds sir. And moreover, there's not enough room in here to place so many beds."

"Then why have you admitted them?"

"Who am I to decide who gets admitted sir? R.S. sir sent papers—what could I do?"

"What else can we expect from your R.S. sir! Just scribble something on a piece of paper. Isn't there any discipline left in this hospital anymore? Send everyone home tomorrow, every last one of them."

"Sir, none of them walked in on foot. They have been carried in on stretchers."

"Then put them back on those stretchers and dump them in the ditches outside. Every single one of them is going to die. They don't have to die in here."

"R.S. sir says he sends only those patients who have to be admitted. Every one of them is critical sir!"

"I know who is critical and who is not! There's no room for them in the hospital—where do you want to keep them? There's not enough space on the floor to walk. There are patients lying in the corridors. Not enough doctors, not enough medicines. If you go on this way you'll send patients to my bedroom some day. Any patient who is not going to die within one hour must be sent him home. You understand? One hour."

"Even if we did that we'd be short of space, sir" The man on duty said innocently, scratching his face.

The doctor uttered an unsure "Hah!" and walked towards the corner where another patient was lying on the floor. Bending, he said, "Who's this kid?" No sooner had he spoken than a black-bearded man sitting there began to wail loudly, "Sir, he's my son, sir, got run over by a train. My only child, sir . . . "

"He got run over by a train? And he didn't die! Why did you bring him to the hospital?"

"He lost a leg, sir."

"A leg? That's not too far from the head. How did he miss it?"

On hearing this, the man suddenly stopped weeping, wiped his tears and kept staring at the doctor.

The doctor said, "Remove that piece of cloth from his leg, let me have a look."

The man removed the cloth, exposing a bandaged stub near the boy's thigh, still dripping with blood. The doctor turned around and said, "What medicines has he been given?" Then he glanced through the prescription and said, "Let's see if he survives the night."

Finally it was Zamiruddi's turn. He was at the north-east corner, near the wall. Grinding all his teeth, the doctor said, "What about you?"

Zamiruddi once again cackled like a duck, but the doctor couldn't hear a word. With his hands on his hips, he bent over Zamiruddi and asked with a mocking smile, "What?"

Gathering all his strength, Zamiruddi managed to utter a few words, "My leg, sir!"

"What about it?" The doctor bent further, observed his leg closely and said, "Hmmm." Then, without a single word, he left with his entourage.

As the night grew darker, the uniformed nurses went from bed to bed. Zamiruddi leaned against the wall and shut his eyes. His legs kept sliding along the floor. He managed to stretch his swollen leg in front of him and began thinking of death. At one point, when the wound on his foot seemed to jump up and bite him, he surmised that death must be lying in wait within the wound. Zamiruddi remembered that wintry morning—he had wrapped a gamchha around his body to protect himself from the chilly wind, picked up his old sickle and stepped out when, suddenly, a sharp and strong thorn pierced the sole of his foot.

He had felt as though something sharp had been drawn across his brain. Going down on one knee, he had examined the wound. As he had tried to pry the thorn out with his massive fingers, it had snapped in the middle. Not a single drop of blood had oozed out, the insides had hurt just a tiny bit, and something had seemed to scrape his brain twice more. Zamiruddi had risen to his feet, unwrapped his gamchha and tied it firmly around his waist, earned seven rupees by putting up a fence around his master's land, gone to the market, bought some rice, come home and had a satisfying meal with his wife and three children. That night, even sleeping with his wife had felt special, and he had completely forgotten about the thorn.

It was difficult to tell exactly how many days had passed after that fateful wintry morning when Zamiruddi noticed that a significant amount of pus had accumulated around the point where the thorn had pierced his foot, and that the region around it had turned white and hard. It hurt, though just a little, and only when he pressed it hard. He and others like him often had to face situations like these—they hardly bothered about it. So he went to the barber and requested him to bring out the piece of thorn that had lodged itself in the flesh. If only the man had said he was busy! But he wasn't, and he gathered his razor, tweezers, nail-slicers, etc., and set to work. Had he succeeded in drawing out the thorn? Zamiruddi never found out. Nor did he know that the good old village barber had slit open the small wound, rummaged around within the pus-filled hole and unwittingly left a trace of death behind. And then one afternoon, he started feeling a bit feverish, and his head felt heavy too. That very night, his entire leg swelled up. By the morning, he himself realised that he wouldn't be able to survive. But then Zamiruddi simply couldn't afford to die either. As he lay on the veranda of his hut, he saw the morning rise from the horizon all the way up to the top of the sky, he saw the dry wind blowing over his yard, kicking up a cloud-like dust storm. There wasn't a single grain of food at home, the earthen oven lay unlit at the far end of the veranda. Zamiruddi could not go out in search of work, and as a result, the oven would remain unlit through the day. Everything seemed hazy, and he couldn't think any further.

Some people seemed to be hoisting him into a bullock cart. A sugarcane field and the blazing heat—he barely remembered anything else now. Zamiruddi opened his eyes and found a strong white light flooding the entire room, a white cloud of dust swirling around, and not a single bed visible any more. Was he dying? He caressed his swollen leg once—it felt blunt and heavy. So he punched it with his fist and at once he felt a hammer blow on his heart, which began to beat very fast. Pinching the skin of the leg, he realised that it still hurt. He wondered how exactly it would feel when he was dying.

"Oh!" A soft whisper emerged through his breath. Zamiruddi opened his eyes and looked around.

A man jumped down from the bed in front and sneaked up to him.

"What's your name?" the man whispered.

"Oh!" Zamiruddi whispered again.

"You haven't brought any sheets, have you?"

Zamiruddi shut his eyes once again.

"O Chacha! What's your name?"

Zamiruddi heard the man now, and realised that he still had some time left.

"My name? My name is Zamiruddi."

"You didn't bring any sheets? Or a quilt or something?"

"No." Zamiruddi's responses came in whispers.

"Take this pillow and lie down."

"Let it be."

The man pulled a pillow down from his bed without moving from the spot and said, "Everything has been fixed here. You walk in through those doors, and you're bound to die. There's no way you are getting out alive." He smiled like an innocent child, his teeth shining in the bright light. "So I always say it's best to get some sleep before you die. What's the point of suffering like this?"

Zamiruddi didn't reply.

"My name is Rashed, and like you, I've also come to the hospital to die."

Zamiruddi barely understood what the man was trying to say.

"What has happened to you?" He asked the man blankly.

"I'll tell you before I die. Now, lie down and try to get some sleep." With these words, Rashed jumped back on his bed.

Zamiruddi tried to pull up the pillow and lie down. But he couldn't move his swollen leg. Eventually he placed the pillow by the wall and rested against it. Soon he began to doze off. After some time, there was some movement on the bed near his head. Zamiruddi opened his eyes and looked up. The man on the bed was sitting upright. His pale face looked strange in the bright light. His eyeballs were popping out of their sockets, he clutched his belly and screamed out, "Oh god . . . it's killing me . . . oh . . . hey . . . no . . . that's it . . . yes, yes, . . . that's . . . it hurts . . . "

A nurse went up to him, asking, "What's the matter?"

"I think I'm going to die."

"Keep quiet and lie down."

"It hurts like hell . . . I'm going to die."

"You were fine all this while, what happened all of a sudden?"

The man exploded in rage. "A dog bit my ass . . . get out of here . . . get out!"

As soon as the nurse walked away, another man lying three beds away began quite calmly, "Wah wah wah . . . very good . . . all right, all right . . . come on now, come on, come to me . . . come to me, you bastard . . . show me what you can do . . . "

Then he drummed up a beat below the lower end of his belly and continued, "Is that all you can do, my boy? Is that all you can do? Come on, come on . . . I'm waiting . . . "

The nurse walked up to him and stood by his side. The man continued to mock his own pain. "Oh ho ho ho . . . ee hee hee hee . . . yes, yes, don't I know your tricks . . . come on, hit me . . . I'll stick it up your ass tonight . . . "

The man began to gasp for breath, clutching the mattress in a desperate search for some relief. Tears began to roll down his cheeks, but still he clenched his teeth and continued to curse at the source of his agony. "Son of a bitch . . . I know what you can do . . . oh yes, I do . . . I'll have your mother tonight . . . "

The nurse asked, "Does it hurt very badly? Try to lie down."

Groans and wails began to emerge from various parts of the room. There had been silence till now, but all sorts of horrid sounds began to be heard. The man near Zamiruddi's head continued to squeal like a pig, showing no intention of stopping any time soon. Zamiruddi managed to cover his own ears to shut out the deafening sound. The man three beds away now began to weep, "Show me what you have, show me . . . eee hee hee heeeeee . . . ooo hooo hooo hooooo . . . wah wah wah . . . no wait, wait, noooo . . . " The man whose son had been run over by a train began to beat his breast and wail once again. As the entire room slowly began to sink under waves of human agony, the nurses darted around gnashing their teeth and admonishing the patients, "Shut up, shut your mouth I say . . . what the hell are you doing? Shut up!"

The doctor with the pockmarked face entered his room at nine o'clock in the morning and settled down in his chair. The first thing he did was to summon Rashed. Rashed walked into the room to find the doctor's eyes smiling. Extending the smile to his lips the doctor said, "What are you going to do about your case?"

"What can I do? You are the ones who know what to do." Rashed looked surprised.

"Yes, of course, but then," the doctor winked, "you are a learned man, we can hardly do anything without your consent."

"Wah! I'm the patient, the sick one . . . you're the doctor . . . do whatever you think is right."

"Take a seat." The doctor pointed at a chair. "It's true that we doctors are supposed to do everything, but not in this country, you understand? Not in this country. I'm taking care of two wards here. I'm the only remaining professor in surgery around here. Do you have any idea how many patients there could be in these two wards? Just do a quick calculation and tell me. Those lying on the bed, those lying on the floor, those lying outside in the corridors, and then those hundreds of men, women and children flocking in from the villages, those who are on their way here—do include all of them in your calculations. Now tell me how many of these patients need surgery right now. How many operations would I have to perform in a day? Rotten gangrenes, punctured ulcers, chopped off legs and arms and what have you, burst hernias and appendices—which of these operations can I postpone?"

When the doctor leaned back in his chair and smiled softly with these words, he didn't seem such a bad person after all.

He continued. "Not one, do you understand, not a single one can be delayed. Each of them needs to be done now—right now! And I'm sure you know what the preparations are for a surgical operation. Blood, stool, and urine examination, a flawless X-ray, sufficient blood in the bank, elaborate arrangements and precautions for anaesthesia, etc., etc. . . . etc. In fact, why don't you come with me, let me show you around? You should see the condition of the operation theatre. And amidst all this, I also have to teach at the college. You tell me, what can I do?" The doctor looked at Rashed with irritation, but summoned a smile to his lips quickly and shrugged. "Therefore, there's no treatment in this country. The scalpels, the scissors, the knives—everything is in bad shape, everything is old. And with these damaged tools, all I can do is draw the mask over my face, shut my mouth and continue to operate upon one patient after another. What else do you expect me to do? Some die before the operation, some die on the operation table. Forget about that, consider this. A patient who needs to be operated on right away is being taken to the OT fifteen days later. Yes, fifteen days. How . . . how do you expect him to survive?"

Rashed spoke after a long pause. "Isn't there any other doctor here?"

"Transfers, transfers!" The doctor said hopelessly. "From one town on the periphery to another. Not from the centre to the periphery, mind you. In other words, not from Dhaka to here, but from here to another small town. No one wants to come from Dhaka to the periphery, and only a fortunate few are transferred from here to Dhaka. So what options are we left with? Keep going round and round and round—from one town to another and then to another, from one periphery to another. I know of at least two doctors—in this very hospital—who have gone on a long leave of absence in protest against such unfair transfers. They will neither accept the transfer nor decline it. Therefore, they can't be replaced either. So you see, unless these transfers can be stopped with canvassing and so on, this deadlock will continue and things will not improve."

"Why don't these doctors go where they are posted? They did know that the job meant transfers, didn't they? They should go."

The doctor grinned to expose two pearl-white rows of teeth and said, "It's easy for you to say that. But why? Why should they go? You think they'll give up their private practice over here and go to a new place? How much does the government pay us in salaries? We're doing this job because we have to—but let me tell you that it is impossible to manage a household on a government salary. And do you have any idea how much a private practitioner earns every month? Some of them are rolling in money—lakhs and lakhs! So? Let's say someone has set up his practice, slowly built a reputation, and is just beginning to settle down as the practice is picking up—and suddenly he is slapped with a transfer notice. And where to? Another remote town. You tell me, who benefits from this? What good can come of something like this? Isn't this the perfect way to unsettle people and disturb their lives? If there's a good doctor in a town, then at least some people will get proper treatment, if not at the hospital then definitely at the doctor's private clinic. And for those who don't have the money, there's no treatment anyway in this wretched country—I already explained that to you. Do you know why the doctors in Dhaka do not want to come to these towns? Money! Plain and simple."

"But they can also get transferred. Why don't they?" Rashed feigned innocence.

The doctor smiled. "Dhaka's professors getting transferred? Hah! That would be the day! The whole country has gone to the dogs, you understand? Listen, I have seen quite a few professors in Dhaka who have grown beards, greyed them, and then shed them too! All this while living and working and minting money in Dhaka! Everything is possible in this country—everything you can imagine, and everything you can't. They say everyone in the government's decision-making bodies is highly intelligent. But once a decision is taken, you'll inevitably realise that even an ass could have done better. And then, dig a little deeper, and you'll soon realise that it's you who is the ass, that you've always been an ass, and that the decision has a hidden significance! Hidden, completely hidden, you understand? Every single jackal in this country is the king, and he wants to rule the land. Everyone knows everyone else, everyone's hand is in everyone else's pocket." The doctor laughed like a jackal! And then he rubbed the grin off his face once again and said, "You tell me how you want me to handle your case. I'd suggest you get out of here." "But if you don't operate now, then I'll be in trouble later, won't I?"

"Correct!"

"Well then?"

"Why else do you think I'm asking you? Oh, what a mess! Had you not been an educated individual, I would have thrown you out of here by now, or plunged a knife into your flesh. The trouble is that you are educated! You see?"

"Well then, assume that I'm a stupid and gullible man," Rashed said calmly.

"You wouldn't have said that had you been stupid or gullible!"

"So what can I do now?" Rashed's voice was steeped in despair.

"Listen," said the doctor with a grave expression and a frown, shiny beads of sweat trickling from the pores on his face. "If you'd have come to me at my private clinic, I'd have taken at least two thousand takas from you, not a paisa less. But I can't do that, because you've admitted yourself in this hospital. So, I'm not getting any money anyway, but I can always offer some free advice, can't I? So listen, if we don't chop off that thing of yours, you aren't going to die, at least not right away, but if we do . . . "

"If we do?" Rashed asked curiously.

"You know, bleeding, etc.—we'll have to sever some of your nerves, your face might be permanently distorted—I mean, there's always some risk in such surgery, you see?"

"What would you have done had I been someone else?"

"I would've chopped it off without asking even once. If nothing else, I'd have gained a new experience. Perhaps the patient would have died on the operation table itself, but they die every day anyway."

"Please operate on me too."

"Are you sure?"

"Yes."

The doctor stared at Rashed for a minute or two. Then he blinked, wiped the sweat off his face and said, "Very well."

Rashed left the room quickly and returned to the ward. The room was now absolutely quiet. The patients were either sitting up or lying. Someone was chewing on a loaf of bread, his dying eyes looking around. Rashed found it difficult to believe that these were the same people who had created the uproar last night. Zamiruddi was half-lying against the wall in one corner. Rashed walked up to him. His swollen leg seemed like a thick block of grey wood. It was quite evident that he couldn't move it even if he wanted to. Although they had not been around in the night, the blue flies had not lost their way and had returned in the morning. Rashed continued to stare at Zamiruddi. Like his face, even his beard had turned pale and colourless. His thick fingers seemed limp now. Rashed suddenly had a terrible urge to scream at him and ask him what on earth he was doing here. Why had he come to die here? Perhaps in response to his silent scream and unpronounced questions, one of Zamiruddi's eyelids trembled a little to let Rashed know that he hadn't succeeded in dying yet.

Somewhere in the middle of the rows of beds towards the southern wall, a patient remarked as he gnawed on his bread, "How come this bread smells of shit? I have never seen bread that smells of shit!" He raised the half-eaten loaf in his hand towards the light, frowned and tried to examine it closely.

The man was dark and lanky. He worked for the police, but had a Hindu string of beads around his neck. Something was wrong with his groin. Talking to Rashed a few days ago, he had announced to everyone around him, "We are staunch Hindus, you know? We're bound to desecrate our faith in a hospital, but we can't help it. Then again, I work for the police—the spine of the nation."

He turned the bread over and around again and again, observing it minutely. "I can bet my life there's shit in this! All my life I've eaten bread, I've never . . . o ho ho ho . . . I'm sure I've desecrated my faith after all . . . "

A stout fair police officer remarked from the adjacent bed, "Shut up! Your faith says it's good to eat cow dung, doesn't it? What's wrong with our dung then?"

"But still, a man shall not have another man's dung," the man responded in poetry with fiery eyes. Then he turned around to face the rest of the room and said bitterly and offensively, "Thieves and robbers, sir, thieves and robbers. Every last one of them. And why not, I say? When the entire country is rife with thieves and robbers, how can this hospital alone have men of good morals?"

Three beds away, a man covered in sores said innocently, "You would know these thieves quite well, wouldn't you sir? You're in the police, after all!"

"Not a single bad word about the police, I warn you!" The Hindu policeman widened his eyes and raised his voice. "We should all remember that even a policeman is a human being. Like anyone else, he too has a wife and children at home. Thieves, robbers, murderers, politicians—basically the scum of the earth . . . a policeman exists because these people exist. Heh heh . . . it's not a joke, you see? And what does this hospital go and do to a policeman like me? I'll tell you . . . "

The man continued to scream his lungs out. He turned his head, threw his hands up in the air and said, "First of all, faith, religion. I'm a Hindu, sir, a staunch, orthodox Hindu. I don't have fish or meat outside my home. And what do they serve here? Shit on bread, shit in the rice. Where do they get so much shit, you tell me? Look, put grit in the food, put mud in the food, put pebbles in the food, we don't mind, I mean why would we? You've been putting these things in our food forever, have we ever complained? But why put shit in the food?"

"Waaack thooo!" The patient in sores spit on the floor.

"All right, fine, fair enough." The policeman didn't seem like he intended to shut up anytime soon. "You say you serve chicken. Now tell me, which part of the chicken looks or tastes like this, no, tell me! This cannot be chicken. But then the more important question is, what is it? Is it dog meat?"

"Dear lord!" Three or four patients yelled out. None of the hospital staff was present.

"You don't know a thing!" The police officer retorted. "It's synthetic meat. Imported from America!"

"Very well, let's move on." The policeman resumed his tirade. "What do you think they did to me three days ago? I must tell you sir, I'm here for a piles operation. And then they found this nasty boil in my groin, it's swollen and all. They took me to the operation theatre three days ago. I thought they would take care of the piles. But no! They asked me to stay still and keep quiet, flung me on a cold table, two bastards walked in and grabbed my legs and arms. I kept telling them, it hurts, it hurts, but no one seemed to care! No injection, no nothing, suddenly a butcher of a man came out of nowhere and plunged a huge knife down there! Just like slaughtering a cow, I tell you! One of them even had the guts to tell me, shut up, if you scream again we'll bring out your dong and chop that off too!"

Standing next to Zamiruddi, Rashed listened to the man's plight. The coolness of the morning was rapidly giving way to the heat of the day. Strong gusts of warm wind blew into the room every now and then. Tall blades of grass stood dead in the large square courtyard in the middle of the hospital building. All that was required was a flame. The thought began to circle inside Rashed's head again and again, like a trapped bird. He would have to gather everyone—everyone. He turned his eyes to Zamiruddi's numb, rotting, swollen stump of a leg. Zamiruddi was sleeping. Bit by bit, the external world was shutting down to him. Gather everyone, live amidst everyone, mingle with everyone, just like a fish dives into the depths of a river. A strong flame seemed to burst out of Rashed's eyes for a moment, he screamed out all of a sudden, "Chacha, Chacha! Do you hear me?"

Zamiruddi lay motionless, not responding. His swollen leg lay beside him, flies hovering all over the rotting flesh. His head was bent over his chest. Something screamed inside Rashed's head once again. "You belong to the middle class, you belong to the ordinary bourgeois, the revolution is not your enemy, but you can wait for it. You don't mind if it comes a little late. But this man—this poor farmer, this poor labourer—he can't afford to wait a moment longer, he needs a revolution now, right now! If the revolution comes now, he lives. If it comes a couple of days later, he dies. If you can explain this simple fact to him, you'll find him opening his eyes and fighting for his life."

Rashed was getting more and more frustrated by the minute. He yelled again, "Chacha, o Chacha—how are you?"

Zamiruddi let out a short deathly rasp, and then, with great effort, managed to open his eyes. His vision was hazy and unclear.

The policeman had finished with his speech a short while earlier. The ward was silent again. Only a faint groan came from somewhere. Once again a warm breeze blew through the room. As Rashed turned back, his eyes met those of an old man a couple of beds away. The man was sitting up, supporting himself with a pillow. He was bare-bodied, the bones on his shoulders jutting eerily. His brittle skin shook with every breath he took. His eyes were so yellow that the scorching rays of the strong sun outside faded in comparison. The man glanced at the sky once or twice and then addressed Rashed in a trembling voice, "I've been here a long time, my boy. Not because I want to live, but because I want to die. But death won't come to me. Such a big and famous hospital—and they can't even help me die! I even tried leaving the hospital—but this wretched country is just like this hospital, it couldn't help me die. If only you knew how painful it is not to be able to die! Everyone tries to live, they flock to the hospital in order to live, and I've come here to die. But I can't. Yet just a few days ago a colic patient from the ground floor walked out of his ward in the middle of the night, went to the mango tree in the backyard, hanged himself from one of its branches and left the world. And here I am! Come, see for yourself . . . over there. See that small mango tree? And that branch over there—not very high up? That one! I saw his naked body hanging from that branch, swaying in the wind, at the crack of dawn."

The old man's voice was hollow. As he continued speaking, Rashed's blood began to boil. His eyes turned red, he clenched his fists and shouted, "Shut up! Shut up!"

Undeterred, the old man continued speaking calmly. "And then the other day, a fox came out of the tall grass and took a newborn baby away from its sleeping mother, and then it . . . "

Rashed gnashed his teeth and yelled, "Shut up!"

The policeman stared at the old man with his mouth agape. But the old man was unstoppable now. He made an effort to convey his final point, "But not once did I have even half a chance to die. These idiots can't even let me die in peace. Lord, I can't even walk up to that mango tree!"

The old man screwed up his eyes, brows, forehead, face—practically everything—but he simply couldn't summon tears to his eyes. They say that as one grows old the tear ducts begin to shrivel and dry up. Everyone in the room remained silent, and only the loudmouth policeman continued to grumble. "What kind of a hospital is this, eh? Can't even kill people properly! Shame on these people, shame on them!"

Clad in a half-sleeved shirt and a dirty, flimsy lungi, the old man from the previous day entered the room. Rashed recognised him immediately. This was the man who had dragged Zamiruddi across the room yesterday. He was now scanning the room, looking for Zamiruddi, whom he couldn't see from where he was standing. As he walked into the room, a woman entered through the door behind, with three little boys in tow. Rashed watched the group keenly. The woman, in particular, surprised him a lot. She had a huge frame, a strong and broad mud-laced pair of jaws, a mud-laced face, a mud-laced pair of wrists, and cracked and dusty pillar-like legs. She stepped into the room and followed the old man around. Her three children trailed behind her, looking around wide-eyed.

The old man had spotted Zamiruddi by now. He called out to the woman, "There he is. I think he's sleeping." Walking past Rashed, he stopped next to Zamiruddi and called out softly, "Zamiruddi, Zamiruddi, look who's come to meet you . . . look!"

There was no response. Stooping, the old man shook Zamiruddi by his shoulders, screaming at the top of his voice, "Zamiruddi, Zamiruddi!

Look, my boy, open your eyes and see . . . your wife and sons have come to see you."

The woman stood still at a distance, watching her husband, her eyes dull and lifeless. She fixed her gaze on Zamiruddi. The youngest child promptly thrust his little finger inside his mouth and sucked on it with great contentment. After being shaken several times more, Zamiruddi opened his eyes very, very slowly. Relieved, the old man touched his arm, but stepped back with a start.

Rashed asked, "What is it?"

The old man raised his eyebrows and said, "Sir! Fever, sir! He's burning!"

By now Zamiruddi's eyes were wide open. The woman had bent over him. But even when he saw her Zamiruddi's eyes showed no glimmer of recognition. On the contrary, they began to close once more, whereupon the old man rushed back to him and screamed, "Zamiruddi! Look, your wife! Your sons are here too . . . look!"

Without saying a word or even trying to speak, Zamiruddi slowly raised his right hand with great effort and placed it lightly on his swollen leg. It looked like a thick huge plum mallet now, which would explode any moment. Rashed saw the woman bend further over Zamiruddi, and as she lowered her face to his, she placed her palm on the wall to support herself. Her huge breasts touched Zamiruddi's chest, her strong neck hunched, her eyes open and still, her mud-laced face now inches away from Zamiruddi's nose. And then finally, her eyes managed to look into the extinguished eyes of her husband's. Her lips were still clamped together, with not even the faintest trace of movement on them—only the sound of her heavy breathing could be heard. Rashed rummaged around in his mind for words spoken and understood by humans, and, quite involuntarily, took a couple of steps towards the dying man and his wife. But the woman didn't utter a single word.

With the briefest of sparks, the light in Zamiruddi's eyes went out again.

The doctor was still sitting in his room. Rashed walked up to his table. As the doctor looked up from the documents on the table, Rashed asked him directly, "Have you examined the man who has come in with the swollen leg?"

The doctor smiled amiably. "Yes, I have."

"What's the situation?"

"Gangrene has set in."

"What needs to be done?"

"He needs surgery immediately—this very moment. Whatever has rotted needs to be amputated."

"And what if the surgery doesn't take place today?"

The doctor smiled amiably once again. "I can see you're upset!"

Rashed raised his voice. "Please tell me, what happens if the surgery doesn't take place today?"

"He's going to die, of course!"

"Are you going to operate on him today?"

"No, it's not possible today."

"How about tomorrow?"

"No, tomorrow's not possible either."

"Will you do it after he dies?"

"Ah, why are you getting upset? There's no operation after death, only a postmortem."

Rashed could hear the gnashing of his own teeth. Smashing his right fist into his left palm, he said, "You are going to operate on him today."

For the third time, the doctor smiled amiably and said in a calm, relaxed voice, "There are several others waiting to die today, I can't possibly turn my attention to him. My axe would lose its sharpness."

With an earth-shattering scream, Rashed said, "You'll have to operate on that man today."

The doctor's face turned from round to square. His small, ugly eyes seemed to be burning as he screamed back, "Not because you are saying so. Get out of here. There are rules in this hospital, and I'm going to follow them. Go now. I do what I can do, and whatever I can't possibly do, I don't—it's as simple as that."

Rashed saw the old man accompanying the woman with the three children walk into the doctor's room. He went all the way up to the doctor's table and seemed to gather his thoughts for a moment or two. Then he looked at the doctor and said calmly, "Sir, we want to take the patient with the swollen leg home."

The doctor sat motionless in his chair. He seemed to have turned into a block of stone.

The old man said once again, "We want to take him home, sir. His family has come to take him home."

In a low voice, the doctor said, "Why?"

"We are taking him home, sir!"

The doctor suddenly seemed to tremble from head to toe. "Come back in a couple of days, you can take him home then. Go now."

Hesitating, the old man lingered. But the woman cast a cold look at the doctor and turned around. With a sudden jerk, she picked up the thumb-sucking little boy into her arms, grabbed the arm of one of the other children and walked out of the room. Rashed stepped out to find the little group climbing down the stairs.

THE
CAGE

Sarojini gasped for breath as she reached the bottom of the stairs. Too cold. Broken edges. Mossy. Too slippery. Like a road that leads to one's downfall and takes one to hell. She concluded that there was no way she could climb those steps. And then the sound of dewdrops came, and with it came the sound of the sitar. Sarojini groaned in pain and yelled, "Get the light, what on earth are you doing over there? Get the light quickly—I can't see a thing here." The sitar stopped singing. She yelled again, "Bring the light."

Ambujaksh was sitting on the terrace with the sitar in his lap and the air of a maestro, clearly not willing to be disturbed or interrupted. As Sarojini managed to make the perilous climb and stepped on the terrace, he looked at her in the light from the lantern and smiled a foul smile. He had prickly bristles on his face, his grey hair sticking to his forehead. The old peepal tree had cracked the wall and towered over the terrace. Its dark shadow danced around them now.

"Come, sit." Ambujaksh indicated a spot on the mat next to him and sent the most cordial of invites.

"No, I've got work to do."

"Sit for a while. I've got something important to tell you. Come, sit for a few minutes."

"Important? If it's so important, come downstairs and tell me."

"You must be wondering whether I'm thinking of you as one of those courtesans, aren't you?"

Sarojini's wizened hand shot up in the air like a snake that had been poked.

"That's it, I'm leaving."

"Give me some paan, will you?"

"We've run out of paan."

"Why don't you get them from the shop?" Ambujaksh put his arms around his wife's waist like a man drunk to his gills.

His feigned intoxication was enough for Sarojini to vomit all the bitter poison that she had been saving inside her for weeks now. Like shots of bitter gall, her words hit Ambujaksh. "Let me go, let me go right now."

One of her front teeth had fallen off the other day. When she talked, the foulest of smells came from her mouth, along with a shower of saliva. Ambujaksh let her go quickly.

"Send someone to the shop to get some paan," he implored again.

"I don't have money. There's no one at home."

"Where's Surya?"

"He'll be back after midnight."

"You talk like a stage announcer!" Ambujaksh guffawed at his own joke. Without wasting any more time, Sarojini cast a stern glance at him, picked up the lantern and walked away.

Ambujaksh's sitar called out to Sarojini in a tragic tune, "Don't go, my love, don't go, for I need you now."

But Sarojini disappeared down the stairs. Ambujaksh smiled a wry smile and concentrated on his sitar. The notes filled the darkness as the dewdrops fell, the melody circled around in the terrace, and on finding an opening down the flight of stairs, it floated along that dark space, over the heads of the sleeping pigeons and entered the empty rooms.

This was how Ambujaksh had been playing the sitar lately. He had picked it up after twenty years. But then, twenty years ago he used to play the sitar quite differently—as if it played itself, as if it was grateful to be in Ambujaksh's lap. And then, he had stopped playing. Ever since he started practising homoeopathy, he stopped playing. Homoeopathy was not easy. It needed his full concentration. But be it homoeopathy or allopathy, these days no one wanted to pay anymore. He would get a couple of takas if the patient had recovered, that too if he was lucky. Or perhaps a few kilos of rice. Or a few vegetables. Therefore, let alone serious ailments like typhoid, pneumonia, tuberculosis, etc., if he were to learn enough homoeopathy to cure just a stomach ache or a running nose, he would have to sacrifice his sitar. His aged father came into his room smoking his hookah one night and said, "It's a pity you stopped playing that thing. Even a madman can be cured by such music alone. The evenings used to be lovely. Why did you stop?"

Ambujaksh could only say, "What other option do I have, tell me? The land is all gone. You are too weak to do any work any more. I have to think about the children too."

"But still, homoeopathy?"

"What else can I do?"

"What about a school? A tol of sorts? After all, we have a trove of knowledge within the family, passed down from father to son, generation after generation."

Ambujaksh stopped what he was doing and looked up at his father. An ancient hookah in his hand, the thick dirty bunch of thread hanging around his neck—they must have been sacred at some time—and those dull, lifeless eyes. He said: "How much have you earned in your entire life? Tell me one thing you have earned? Going door to door in those wooden clogs, helping people with their rituals, what have you got out of all those years of priesthood? We can't do that any more, now they have created Pakistan, the country's been split into two. What do we do now?"

Therefore the sitar was banished to one of the dark rooms in the west, and there it hung from the wall in solitary confinement. Ambujaksh shifted his focus to diarrhoea, seizures, indigestion, menstrual irregularities, colic, frequent urination and such other national ailments of Bengal.

"Are things working out for you?" His father was standing at the doorway.

Ambujaksh was counting coins, jingling them deliberately. He frowned as he looked up. He looked baffled for a moment, as if he had not recognised the man at the door. Then he resumed counting and said, "Well, more or less. Sometimes people don't pay. Take Zameer Sheikh for instance—his son's spleen became so enlarged it popped out of his body. When he was brought to me the little boy was sitting on his own spleen! Not a very conducive situation to ask for a fee. Or take Padma Pishi, she walked up to me and thrust two small mangoes in my palm and said, 'That's all I have, son. Please forgive me. I'm in pain.' That's how things are, you know."

Pulling twice on his hookah strongly, Kaliprasanna coughed, trembling from head to toe. "Hiron (Ambujaksh's pet name), you're growing old too, my dear boy. If only I could help you somehow, even if that means having to die."

How long can one count coins, really? Ambujaksh looked up and saw his father walking away in the blazing sun. A crow perched on the cornice cawed. Ambujaksh called out to his father, asking him to come back. He returned, grabbing Ambujaksh's heart and wringing it like a butcher. "Hiron, son, can you give me two annas? But if it's a problem let it be."

"Why do you need it?"

"I thought I'd get a shave. My hands tremble, I can't hold the razor straight."

Ambujaksh threw two coins at the old man. "All right, go."

The wooden clogs worked up a depressing rhythm on the ground. The blazing sun struck again.

"Who's there?" Ambujaksh said.

"Arun."

"Come here."

No one came.

"Arun, I said come here."

"Later. I'm going out now, I'm getting late."

Sarojini entered after some time. When Ambujaksh complained to her about their son's attitude, she defended him like a lawyer. "Why, what do you want from him?" Ambujaksh thought hard for several minutes but couldn't remember. In fact, he could barely remember anything.

"There are hills over there, right?" Sarojini leaned towards Ambujaksh, widened her eyes like a sick girl and said, "That's what you said the other day. If there are no hills, we won't go there. My father used to say . . . "

"Hills? There are no hills," Ambujaksh said, chewing a mouthful of rice. "You can see hills from Nalhati, the Chotanagpur Range. Very beautiful—like large blue clouds."

"Can't we go there instead?" Sarojini made her demand to her husband through the prettiest of pouts.

"Oh but that's quite far away—twenty or thirty miles, at least. That's where the Santhals live."

"In that case, tell them that you don't want to go there. We're taking so much trouble to move. Once we get to India and settle down somewhere, we won't get a chance to shift from one town to another whenever we wish to. If an exchange is taking place, you should grab the opportunity to live in a beautiful place."

"All right, we'll think about it. What's the rush? It's not like we're leaving tonight."

"If we have to go, then let's go as soon as possible, what's the point of lingering? We've lived here all our life—who knows, maybe we won't be able to leave everything behind when the time comes. Everyone is leaving, we'll have to leave too."

We'll have to leave! We'll have to leave!

The words struck at the very core of Ambujaksh's heart. Indeed! We'll have to leave—we'll have to leave everything behind. The cloud-filled skies, the cool roof over the head, the quay by the pond, the white pathway, the sweet smell of the vines, Zameer Sheikh, Padma Pishi—we have to leave our souls behind in each of them, and be reborn in a new land, under a new sun. The blue mountains, the roaring sea—they dance in my mind. Yes, we'll leave too!

Ambujaksh began to rush through his meal.

"Tell me, why don't we go to a place which looks like this one? One where there's a river flowing by, with lots of trees and plants? Perhaps a cool place?" Ambujaksh said. "Then we can see the same birds, the same sky, the same clouds."

"Where do you want to go?"

"Someplace near Nabadweep. And why just Nabadweep? That entire landscape is so much like this place. I've been there—trees and plants all around, lots of cool shade."

"I'm not so sure I'd like to go to the woods. I'd rather we go to a dry place."

"We're building castles in the air, really." Ambujaksh washed his hands and came back into the room. "Three years have gone by, and nothing has worked out. Something or the other keeps coming up. Sometimes there's no one who wants to exchange, and when we do get someone, we can't agree to the terms, or the government comes up with a new rule."

"We'll need a proper brick house, like this one." Sarojini put forward another demand.

"Of course, we've been living in a brick house for such a long time, we wouldn't be able to adjust otherwise. Don't worry, I won't agree to an exchange if it's not a brick house." Ambujaksh was about to leave the room after this assurance, but Sarojini called him back.

"Wait, take the paan. Where's your mind these days?"

"I'll be in the living room. Ask Bhaybla to bring it to me."

"Bhaybla is not at home."

"Where's he gone?"

"No idea. I don't know where he goes."

"You don't know? Why, are you asleep when he steps out? Tell me one thing you know that's happening in this house." Ambujaksh flared up instantly, and the more he shouted, the more his fury mounted.

"What the hell are you here for? The children are turning out to be hooligans of the first order—every one of them! The eldest one has recently discovered the art of shaving. The cheeky bugger has the gall to steal his father's razor! The middle one gets into brawls and fistfights every other day. And you don't even know where the youngest one is. Why on earth should I feed this pen of pigs, tell me."

Sarojini lost her temper too. "Because that's all you can do. For three years you've been jumping up and down with your big plans—we're going to India, we're going to India! And what do you do to make it possible? Homoeopathy! And what have you ever done to bring up the children well?"

The clickety-clack of wooden clogs on the cemented floor rang through the house.

A sudden shriek cut through the air like the sharp blade of a knife in the dark. "Snake, snake!"

Where was this snake? This was not just any snake but Takshak—the king of snakes. The deity of the home. When the emerald-green tiny leaves of the peepal tree had made their way through the north-western wall of the largest and the most beautiful room of the house, almost invisible cracks had begun to appear on the wall. At first, they looked much like the intricate mesh of veins on the peepal leaves. But then, they began to widen. And then, when the monsoons ended, the snake arrived on a cold wintry morning and announced its presence, "Cut cut cut—tokke tokke" and immediately vanished behind the leaves. The roof had cracked open by then, so the room had to be vacated. It was the second son Arun who first saw it in the empty, abandoned room. A large reptile, with greenish spots on its white skin. Arun stepped out of the room looking for a suitable weapon and bumped into his grandfather.

"What's the matter?"

"There's a snake in the room. I'm going to kill it."

"Where? Let me see?"

The old man entered the room and looked at the animal. His eyes narrowed, and creases appeared all over his forehead. He seemed to be gazing at an ancient being. That was all. Then his lips started trembling, and he broke down into tears. "You've had mercy on me, after all! You've come? You've come to my home? Please stay. Live in my humble home."

Wiping his tears, he turned to his grandson. "He's not a snake, my boy. He's the king of snakes. A deity. Don't even think about harming him."

The Takshak had vanished within the foliage of the peepal by then. But it had remained in and around the house ever since. Today, Sarojini came running out of the kitchen on hearing the scream. In the rush, the fire in the lamp in her hand went out. She screamed hoarsely, "Where is it, Arun? Where's the snake?"

"Don't come here. Stay where you are. It's right there, near your feet, in the grass. Don't move—I'll hack it to death today."

Something slithered in the long dry grass with a rustling sound. Sheer neglect had let the grass and the weeds grow almost as high as Sarojini's knees. No one had bothered to cut the grass or clear the weeds in months. Sarojini often wondered, what was the point? They would have to leave soon anyway. She was standing there, trembling, while Arun ran around looking for something to beat the snake with. He looked like a ghost, running from one end of the house to the other in the faint darkness. The dark empty rooms stared back at her in silence. The light in the old man's room had gone out too. Perhaps he had fallen asleep. Or perhaps some ancient memory was haunting him, waging war with his consciousness. And so there was silence in that room too. Ambujaksh was not at home, he had stepped out in the neighbourhood to indulge his habit of chewing tobacco. There was no one else in the house. A strong breeze blew over the grass.

"Look at all these weeds. Arun. Don't go there, I beg you. Listen to me."

"Shut up," a hoarse voice rang out.

"You don't have to kill it, my boy."

"Will you stop nagging and let me do my job?" Arun screamed at the top of his voice, shaking the stick in his hand. He sounded so crass and cruel. Sarojini felt as though it was she and not the snake whose head the stick had descended on.

Arun gnashed his teeth and looked around. "Where are you? Come out, come out, my baby."

"It's gone, it must have run away by now. Come up on the veranda now."

"For heaven's sake, shut up, bitch!" Arun spluttered as he screamed, his eyes blood-red with rage.

Darkness is said to protect a person's dignity. Mother and son couldn't see each other in the dark.

"Hissss!"

"You wretched creature . . . you bit me?"

"It bit you? Did it bite you, Arun?" Sarojini shouted in the dark. "I told you not to go there. What am I going to do now?"

"Shut up. It's bitten me—so what? Why the hell are you barking?"

"Why did you not listen to me, son? What am I going to do now?" Sarojini wailed, beating her breast and tearing at her own hair.

"What's the worst that can happen? I'll die, right? Who wants to live anyway?"

Did homoeopathy offer a cure for snakebites? Ambujaksh could hardly think straight, let alone remember. One moment it seemed to him that a suggested remedy did exist, and the next moment he felt it didn't. Arnica Pulsatilla, Nux Vomica . . . what was it? His father Kaliprasanna was still sleeping in the darkened room. Finally, Ambujaksh did remember that there indeed was a homoeopathic medicine for snakebites—a miracle remedy. Trouble was, he just couldn't remember its name. Ambujaksh considered the situation. Perhaps he had never known the name. Perhaps his knowledge of the subject was incomplete, insufficient. Or perhaps he knew, but had forgotten. Whatever the case may be, all they could do now was the wait for the shaman to arrive. Meanwhile, Arun had started frothing in the mouth. He started wasting away.

"Am I really dying?" Arun muttered in his stupor.

"Arun, don't sleep! Don't sleep, Arun!" Sarojini yelled.

"Arun?" Ambujaksh shook his son by his shoulders. "Try to stay awake."

"I wonder what the blasted fuss is all about." Those were his last words. As dawn broke, Arun died.

"You know what, Sarojini? I've made all the arrangements!"

"What arrangements?"

"For the exchange." Ambujaksh spared an embarrassed smile.

"Heaven alone knows how long you've been telling me that." Sarojini was in the kitchen, busy with her cooking.

"No, no. This time, everything has been fixed. They had come, they've examined all our land and property."

"Did they like it? Sarojini suppressed her excitement successfully.

"Of course they liked it! This house, these trees and plants, the cool shade and greenery all around—where are they going to get all this? The only thing they didn't like was the weeds. They complained of too much weeds and grass. And apparently, the pond needs some work too. And they said, the house is practically gone. If we have to live here, we'll have to chop off those peepal and banyan trees first. Or else the house will fall on our heads one day. So I said, why don't you start over and lay the foundations of a new house when you start living here? It's your house now, your land too. You can build according to your wishes. Then the gentleman asked me, why are you going? So I asked in return, why are you coming?"

"What did he say?"

"The same reasons! No future, no security—all the things we usually say!"

"I'm sure he thinks he'll be the king of the world once he gets here."

"That's what it seemed like. He said he'll build everything afresh."

"I think we should also do the same once we get there."

"Things have come to a state where even if my hair has grown, I'd prefer to wait a little more and get the haircut over there!"

"Where does this gentleman live now?"

"A village near Katoa—Agradweep."

"What a beautiful name!"

"Not just the name, the place is beautiful too. I've been there as a child with my father. I was just a little boy then. White earth, huge fields reaching all the way to the horizon, a train track cutting through it. Kolkata on one side, and Khagda, Azimganj, Nalhati, going all the way up to Bolpur, and then Bardhaman."

Sarojini stopped cooking. It was difficult to pay attention to such day-to-day activities amidst such beautiful descriptions.

"Such a big country!" Ambujaksh continued. "Where do you want to go—Delhi, Agra, Puri, Mathura, Vrindavan? You can easily go anywhere you want to."

"Their house—is it a brick one?"

"Yes, it is. Maybe, I'm not sure. You can go anywhere you want, anywhere at all."

"I don't want to go anywhere. I've managed the household all my life. I'm exhausted now. I'll simply sit quietly and take some rest when we get there. You can't make me work all day any more. Just put aside a small patch of land for me, I'll grow a little garden there—shiuli, bokul, champa, roses—just like the one we used to have all those years ago."

"The children . . . " Ambujaksh muttered and sighed. Sarojini was also about to speak, but she too stopped short. It had been more than a month now that Surya had stopped coming home.

It had been several years that he'd stopped going to college. He was often involved in skirmishes and gang wars. He had five younger siblings. Two of them would sit down to study once or twice. The other three roamed around the fields like unattended cows. They often discussed how their father would put them in a new school when they reached India, how they would get to wear sparkling new clothes.

Clearing his throat, Ambujaksh said, "We'll have to put the children in school. They need proper education. We've not tried to get them to go to school ever since we've been planning to leave."

He sat in silence for some time. Then he said, "There's nothing to be made from homoeopathy these days."

"There's nothing to be made from anything these days," Sarojini answered.

"Yes, I agree."

"So, it's all settled then? All the arrangements have been made?"

"Almost all."

"Almost? But didn't you just say it's final this time?"

"There are lots of things to consider. Many demands to be met—it's not as easy as it used to be."

"When will we go? We're getting old!"

"Yes, we're getting old, aren't we?"

Ambujaksh was lost in his thoughts. The Takshak called out from the branches of the peepal tree, startling him. The cruel afternoon sun was shining brightly. Every blade of tall grass in front of the house was dead.

Now was the time to light the fire! Right now! Ambujaksh said to himself. One matchstick would be enough. The flames would flare up in an instant, easily engulfing everything—the roof, the ceiling, the empty granary, Sarojini's rickety bones—everything. Why don't I do it? Ambujaksh asked himself. I'll set everything on fire. Then I'll hold Sarojini to my breast, and then Baba, Sarojini, Surya, Varun, Kamal, Bhaybla and I—we'll all stand over there and watch the destruction—and then walk into the fire ourselves.

What a horrible thought! Ambujaksh shut his eyes tight and opened them again, rubbing them furiously. He looked up at the peepal tree. How tall and large it had grown! It has even cracked the northern wall. As he stared at the wall, the sun's rays suddenly appeared to turn sharper and more piercing, and the wall seemed to split into two with a cracking noise in front of his very eyes.

"Listen, come here quickly," Sarojini called out to her husband as she entered the room.

"What's the matter?"

"Can't you hear me say come quickly?"

Ambujaksh took his time to shut the lid of the medicine box. He flicked a piece of dust from his dirty dhoti and looked up to find Sarojini gone. As he stepped out and locked the door, he saw Sarojini running towards Kaliprasanna's room. On entering, Ambujaksh's eyes met a strange sight. Sarojini had both her arms around Kaliprasanna, trying her best to pull him up from the floor. Kaliprasanna's eyes were shut.

"What's happened to him?"

"He fell down suddenly. Help me put him on the bed."

Kaliprasanna lay motionless.

Ambujaksh said, "I've lost count of the number of times I've told him not to try anything on his own. He's grown old after all. We're there, he can always call us, it's not like we'll refuse to help. But he just won't listen. Now what? He'll suffer for six months, at least. He must have tripped and fallen."

But on learning from his wife that the old man had not tripped, or that his wooden sandals had not come off either, and that he had simply collapsed for no apparent reason, Ambujaksh stared at his father in shock, as if he had been struck by a bolt of lightning. Finally, he said, "Oh lord! I think . . . he . . . "

"What is it? What's happened to him?"

"Paralysis!"

The Takshak called out at that precise moment. Kaliprasanna opened his eyes and said, "Hiron?"

Ambujaksh walked up to the bed and leant over him. "What is it, Baba?"

"What happened to me, Hiron?"

"Nothing Baba, you fell down, that's all."

"My right side suddenly became numb. My head began to reel, and I . . . "

"These things happen when you're weak. You'll get better soon."

"Hiron . . . I can't move my right hand . . . "

"Don't worry Baba, you'll get better soon."

It seemed Kaliprasanna could neither hear nor see anything.

He began to wail uncontrollably. "Have I been paralysed? Is that what this is?"

Ambujaksh stood at his father's bedside in silence, gazing at the old man. He had not shaved in days, his cheeks were hollow, and his face seemed twisted and ugly because of the paralysis, his words almost incomprehensible.

"A man can't die when he wishes to, Hiron. But he can choose to kill himself if he wishes to. Please kill me my son, I beg of you, please kill me. I'll bless you with all my heart."

"What nonsense!" Ambujaksh began to feel a strong sense of irritation.

"Please give me something, some poison . . . I want to die. I want to die right now. Hiron, my son . . . please Hiron . . . " Kaliprasanna continued to groan unintelligibly.

"If you don't behave yourself, then I'll leave right away."

"Then you tell me what should I do."

"Lie down quietly."

Ambujaksh had always found it strange when old men wept, although he knew quite well that only the aged could weep like little children. But watching an old man weep was far less bearable than watching a child weep, because an old man had the ability to pour a lifetime of bitter experiences into his tears. Kaliprasanna seemed to shed those bitter tears now, and as they began to poison the air of the room, Sarojini covered her face with her sari and sobbed like a ten-year-old schoolgirl. Meanwhile, Surya made a dramatic entry into the scene. His lungi pulled up above his knees, his torso brazenly uncovered, his behaviour coarse and uncouth. He stepped into the room, stared at everyone and said in his characteristic hoarse voice, "What's happened here?"

No one responded.

"Why's everyone standing around like idiots?"

"Your grandfather has been paralysed, Surya'—Sarojini managed to utter the words as she cried.

"He has had what?"

"Paralysis."

"Now that it has happened, why the hell are you all crying like babies?"

His words sounded so crude and inhuman that even Kaliprasanna felt ashamed and stopped crying.

"Give him some of those medicines of yours," Surya stared at his father coldly and hissed cruelly, "till he kicks the bucket."

Then he grabbed Sarojini's arm in a powerful grip and shook it violently. "Give me something to eat. I need to go out."

"Oh, how they bark!" Ambujaksh pricked his ears to listen. It sounded like a thousand jackals baying together. Sarojini had gone downstairs, and the sitar was still on his lap. It had become very cold. And then he heard the call of the Takshak in the dark— Cut Cut Cut! Ambujaksh put the sitar down on the mat, picked up half a brick and walked up to the mammoth peepal tree. He had to watch his step in the dark. The floor of the terrace was riddled with cracks by now, and Ambujaksh knew that some of these cracks were large enough for his feet to go through them.

The part of the terrace near the peepal tree seemed perilously weak. And yet he stared into the darkness of the tree, looking for the Takshak. But all he could see were the faint outlines of the leaves, shaking in the cold wintry breeze. Ambujaksh gave up after several minutes of waiting, tossing the brick away and walking back to the sitar. The moss on the roof had become so thick that Ambujaksh felt he was walking on a soft carpet in the dark. In fact, he had just begun to imagine that he indeed was walking on a carpet, even enjoying the experience, when he lost his footing on a particularly slippery spot and nearly fell on the floor, which brought his dream to a rude end. Ambujaksh felt his heart hammering against the walls of his chest.

Won't Sarojini come back, then? Even as he asked himself this question, Sarojini came upstairs and said, "Come on downstairs, I'm serving you dinner. I have a lot of work."

"Why don't you sit down for a minute, Sarojini?" There was a sense of melancholy in Ambujaksh's voice, which Sarojini didn't fail to notice.

"What's got into you today? Why are you behaving this way?"

"Please sit down for a minute, Sarojini," Ambujaksh repeated like a chant. Sarojini lowered herself to a corner of the mat. Ambujaksh sat in silence for a long time. Finally, he spoke softly.

"We're not going Sarojini."

To get over the insuperable sorrow brought forth by his words quickly, Ambujaksh said with a chuckle, "We tried, but we simply couldn't do it. Nothing worked out. And what would we have gained even if we had gone, tell me. It's the same story everywhere. From whatever little I've heard, it seems we're still getting two square meals a day here, but there people are starving to death."

Sarojini sat in silence.

"To dream of going somewhere is one thing, but to actually go is a different matter altogether. Don't you agree? All these years we've dreamed of going. Now, let's see how it feels when we know that we don't have to go any more." Ambujaksh's voice seemed distant, lost.

"Moreover, everyone here loves us so much, there's so much respect for us. And most important, Baba's condition . . . I mean . . . so long as he's alive . . . "

Ambujaksh didn't really know what else to say. His thoughts were snarled in a giant knot inside his head. Sarojini continued to sit in the dark like a ghost. She had not spoken a word. Not knowing what to do, Ambujaksh picked up the sitar again and quickly threw himself into the waves of the Desh raga.

The beautiful melody was borne aloft by the breeze. The red light of the lantern began to appear redder by the minute. Ambujaksh shut his eyes and moved his head with the rhythm of the music, losing himself in it.

When the shell of the sitar broke into smithereens with a loud sound, Ambujaksh opened his eyes and looked at Sarojini, who had flung away the stick in her hands and picked up the lantern instead. When that shattered with an explosion too, Sarojini advanced towards Ambujaksh.

Ambujaksh screamed into the night, pleading with his wife, "No Sarojini, not me . . . not me . . . not me."

EXCAVATION

The rest house was in a particularly secluded part of the town. Shahed had considered it passable. The skies had been overcast all through the previous day. There had been two or three heavy showers as well. But a clear morning greeted him as he woke up and looked at the sky. He felt good. A thin white fog rising from the ground, the sun peeping out from behind the deep green horizon, where a village was situated. An ordinary sight. So ordinary, in fact, that it could easily be branded 'eternal.' Shahed smiled, his fleshy cheeks, covered by an ungroomed salt-and-pepper beard, twisting in joy. Shahed loaded his toothbrush with paste, began to brush his teeth, and said sleepily: "Muneer! Muneer! How can you sleep so soundly when your ass is bared to the world? Get up!"

Shahed was a seasoned journalist. He'd had a filthy tongue for years. Grasping the end of Muneer's loosely tied lungi between his toes, he jerked it away. "Get up, you son of a bitch, look around you! Look at the beautiful scenes! How can you keep sleeping?"

Muneer sat up with an irritated but imploring expression, pulled up his lungi from somewhere near his knees, tied it around his waist and went back to bed, saying, "Please Shahed Bhai, I couldn't sleep a wink all night because of the heat."

Shahed walked up to the bed, grabbed a pawful of Muneer's hair and tugged at it violently. "And why is that my darling? Why couldn't you sleep? There was no whore beside you, is that why? Get up!"

There could be no more sleep after this. Muneer sat up, rubbing his eyes. He found Shahed's large solemn face dripping with sweat, even at this early hour. He was staring at Muneer with his small, ugly eyes—perhaps he had suddenly remembered that Muneer's wife had left him a few months ago for a rich bureaucrat twice her age. He mouthed a single, almost incomprehensible, word from behind the foam and the brush in his mouth. "Sorry!" There was a frown on his forehead, and his corpulent face was creased with lines, his small eyes almost invisible.

Muneer wondered whether this was how Shahed would look if he were to cry. But the impossibility of such an occurrence made him smile. He said, "Why are you swearing so early in the morning Shahed Bhai?"

"Swearing? What the hell do you know about swearing? You wake up in the morning, you swear for a few minutes—and there you are—your soul's clean and clear, ready for the day ahead. Do you understand?"

"I've heard of cleaning my teeth in the morning, I've heard of clearing my bowels in the morning. But cleaning your soul— I haven't heard of that!"

"Of course you haven't! Who the hell has a soul these days, you tell me? Come on now, hurry up. We've got a lot to cover. I want to get back to Dhaka by tomorrow."

The two men stepped out of the room. The huge field in front of the rest house had been washed in the sunlight by now, but neither of them paid any attention to the sight.

There was almost no food at the rest house. Hotels were not very well equipped in small towns like these. After much effort, all they could find were a few slices of stale toast and four eggs. Shahed asked the boy who had brought the food, "This hen— have you tamed it yet? Does it listen to you?"

The dark-skinned boy looked like an urchin. Baring his red gums and scratching his head in perplexity, he said, "Why sahib, are the eggs too small?"

Shahed bit into his toast: "Never mind. Go get the tea."

They could see a part of the station from where they were sitting—a stretch of the platform, a barbed-wired fence, a couple of abandoned wagons.

When they stepped out after breakfast, they realised that things had taken a nasty turn. The sun was already blazing hot. Soft, reddish, and tender early in the morning, it had turned into a ball of scalding hellfire—looking at it directly was impossible. The cloudless, light blue sky had become a smouldering copper plate. Vapours rose from puddles of dirty muddy water that had collected in the potholes overnight. Shahed was quickly soaked in sweat. He was fat, and Muneer wondered whether he had any flesh left, for he looked like a barrel of fat. Pulling out his hand-kerchief, he wiped his face and neck. The handkerchief was now sodden too—so much so that he didn't feel like stuffing it back into his pocket, and held it in his hand instead.

"I'm an . . . I mean I like the scenic beauty of the countryside, you know," Shahed said, gasping for breath, "but the blasted sun's burning my skin."

"More than the heat, it's the humidity. I think it's going to rain again, Shahed Bhai," said Muneer.

"Shut up with that scientific shit. The sun is cracking my skin and bones, and he says it's going to rain. So let it rain, who's stopping it?"

"But if it rains, they'll have to stop the work. It's such a huge project, so many people're involved. Everything'll come to a halt."

"What an asshole you are! First you say it's going to rain, and now you're saying if it rains . . . make up your mind."

"No, I mean, it might rain. There's a possibility, you know? And if it does, then the work will have to be stopped, which won't be good, right?"

"Why? Is this your father's project? What is it to you if the work stops?"

"You're not getting it, Shahed Bhai. People have started this mammoth project. Do you realise what an important accomplishment it would be if this canal were to be completed, if the common people could be coaxed into finishing the job? This area will see a huge change, and everyone will benefit."

"Then why the hell are you here? You could have stayed back in Dhaka and written in that pathetic newspaper of yours about how the place will flourish if the canal can be built with the help of the people."

"But I have to see it with my own eyes. How can I write till I've seen it for myself? After all, ethical journalism means . . . "

"Shut up!" roared Shahed. "Don't ever mention ethics and journalism and all that bullshit again. You and your ideals! Isn't it good enough that you've got food on your table at the end of the day? Why get yourself into ethics? The entire country's going to the dogs and his highness is talking about ethical journalism!

Heh! Have you seen the pet parrots in those Brahmin households? They're taught to say Radhe-Krishna, Radhe-Krishna! You really want to do ethical journalism? Go stand in front of the parrot and ask her why she says Radhe-Krishna. What does she mean by it? Wait, let me take a piss. Demand an answer—don't let her get away. That's ethical journalism for you, heh!"

They had walked out of the town by now. A large brown field was spread out before them. Despite yesterday's heavy showers, the earth had already dried under the sun. Heat rose from the blackened, scorched ground. They could see a body of water in the distance. There was something over there—either a river or a canal.

Shahed had walked to the side of the road, planted his feet apart and started urinating. Muneer, looking away, said, "Ours is a rural economy, isn't it Shahed Bhai? I mean, everything is in the villages, most of the land in our country is there too. So we have a rural economy—I mean our economy is heavily dependent on agriculture, and . . . "

Muneer turned around to find Shahed buttoning his trousers and walking towards him, staring with those cold, frightening eyes. Muneer licked his dry lips and swallowed. He mumbled, "I mean, I was saying . . . that agriculture is the very backbone of our . . . economy . . . "

"Now if you're done with all your preambles and prefaces, do consider enlightening me about how exactly how you expect the people of the region to benefit from the canal?"

"I don't like fooling around all the time Shahed Bhai." With no arguments left in defence, Muneer tried to display some anger.

"Listen, my friend," said Shahed softly, "you have no idea what exactly is going on here, do you? Nor do you have any idea about what will happen once the project is finished. You're simply shooting arrows in the dark. All I'm saying is that first you need to see things for yourself, you need to know the ground realities—then you can go and write as many lies as you wish to, I won't stop you. I mean, why would I? The entire profession has become just a way to spread lies. Everyone does it. Why, even I do it. Why should you be any different?"

As Shahed wringed his soaked handkerchief a couple of times, thin streams of dirty sweat rolled down between his thick fingers. He wiped his face and neck with the handkerchief once again and exhaled—"Villages! Rural economy! Motherland! Bullshit! It's one bare field after another, either standing bare under the blazing sun, or rotting under flood waters. Enter any damned village and you'll be surrounded by dirty black street urchins—they look like insects, I tell you—every one of them naked, every one of them holding a dented enamel bowl. Grovelling in the mud, getting swept away in the flood, dying of cholera and dysentery. And all you can think of are bombastic words like economy, democracy, bureaucracy, magicracy?"

When they reached the banks of the river, the loudspeakers were blaring a song at deafening volume—I miss you in the night, the world knows not my plight. I'll make you mine, the stars will shine, don't go out of my sight.

With a nasty smile Shahed said, "What the fuck! Stop yelling. You're going to crack that croaking throat of yours."

The root source of the chaos—presumably a gramophone—was nowhere to be seen. Dozens of loudspeakers had been set up.

There was not a single drop of water in the river—none whatsoever. Only the signs of a river flowing through this place in the past remained. The silt had piled up so high that the bed of the river was almost level with its banks. Around five hundred men and women were busy digging.

Shahed studied the scene from a distance. After some time he realised that he was staring blankly. What had happened? His ears were ringing, no doubt thanks to the loudspeakers, but why couldn't he focus on what was going on in the distance? Then he realised that along with his ears, his eyes had also stopped functioning. Hundreds of bare dark-skinned dirty bodies, clad in nothing but loincloth, were digging with spades and pickaxes, filling empty baskets with loose earth and sand, swearing and cussing at each other, crawling around—as if it was all a dream. He had crossed such an enormous field on foot, that too in this sweltering heat. He must have become completely dehydrated by now. His heart was beating faster than usual. He could no longer see clearly in any case, the metallic blaring of the cheap songs being the last straw. Three or four young boys came running up, selling cigarettes, beedis, paan and nuts. Shahed shooed them away with great difficulty. The leader emerged from the crowd with a smile on his face, his feet dragging as he walked up.

"Welcome, welcome! Where are you gentlemen from?" he asked. Wearing a white half-sleeved shirt and pyjamas, he was neatly shaven and wore three rings on three of his fingers, each with a shiny stone in a different colour. He chewed on paan, his lips appearing blood-red, and he walked with the air of a man in charge.

"Just looking around," Muneer said. "We're journalists."

"You're journalists?" The man grinned so widely that his red gums seemed to melt and drip. But he didn't let that happen, slurping the crimson paan-juice back into his mouth and said, "Most welcome, most welcome! You live so far away in the capital. Dhaka! How can you possibly know what an important project we have taken up here in this village? Come with me, I'll tell you all about it, come inside."

In a most casual and disinterested tone, Shahed said, "Go where?"

"Come and see what beautiful arrangements we've made! Five tents have been pitched over there. There's a gramophone playing in one of them. The one next to it is for publicity and propaganda. Three high school students have been brought here—they've been asked to shout slogans and spread the word all day. Yes, all day. Publicity is important, it should never stop. You should write in your papers—the villagers of Bangladesh are not taking it lying down anymore. A revolution has started."

A thin unwavering smile was stuck to the man's face. It seemed to Muneer that he was studying them with his sharp eyes.

"When did your revolution start?" Shahed asked calmly.

"Revo . . . oh the revolution? Let's see . . . ten days or so?"

"Take it down," Shahed told Muneer.

Muneer was about to bring his pad out of his bag when the man said, "But why stand here in the sunlight? Come with me, please, come with me. We'll sit down and talk at length."

Shahed managed to drag his heavy body all the way to a tent with great difficulty under the blazing sun. The tent itself was tattered. It must have been white at some time in the past, but now it was a dirty brown. Gusts of wind blew dust into the tent through the six-inchwide opening at the bottom, making it difficult to breathe. The front of the tent was open, giving a view of the river bed. Hot air was blowing in through the entrance. The grass on the ground inside the tent had been crushed underfoot. Three chairs of mango wood surrounded an old table. Shahed sat down on one of the chairs facing the river bed without waiting for anyone. A small crowd of naked children and beggars gathered around him at once.

"Please, please, take a seat," The man said, the thin smile still stuck to his face.

"All the beggars have been put to work," he said proudly. "Nobody here has to beg any more. Man or woman—everyone who is able-bodied has to work here."

"What about them?" Shahed indicated the beggars.

"We tried, but they simply refused to work. I think we should shoot every single one of them dead."

"Did you take that down?" Shahed shut his eyes and asked Muneer.

Immediately the man snarled, "Get out of here, you filthy pigs, you bastards . . . "

"Take everything down." Shahed was unmoved.

No one spoke for a minute or two. Muneer was sitting with the pen and pad in his hands, but he had not made even a single mark on the paper.

Shahed asked, "How long has this river been dry?"

The man replied, "I've been seeing it this way ever since I was a child, sahib."

"This canal that you plan to dig—how long will it be?"

"Around twelve miles long."

"Will you get water here once it's connected to the river?"

"Absolutely."

Shahed shut his eyes once again. The sun was too strong. The beggars had not moved too far away. A young woman had joined the crowd—she had a little baby in her arms. Her dirty clothes had somehow managed to cover the lower half of her body, but her unusually bloated longish hard breasts were sticking out of her tattered sari. She didn't seem bothered. Instead, she stared at Shahed with large white eyes, a frown of curiosity on her forehead. It seemed to Shahed that the woman was staring at him, but he could have been wrong, because she was slightly squint-eyed. From the corner of his eye Shahed noticed Muneer putting his pen down on the table and licking his dry lips quickly. He looked away in disgust.

"Are all the people working here beggars?"

"No, no! What are you saying, sahib? They're not all beggars."

"Are they working without payment?"

"Well, they will work in exchange of food—that was the plan. After all, this is nation-building. Only when everyone dirties their hands will the nation be able to stand on its feet."

"Where exactly are the nation's feet?" The words slipped out of Shahed's mouth.

"I'm sorry? What are you saying?"

"Never mind. So, no one is being made to work without payment now?"

"They worked without payment for the first one or two days. Everyone was really excited. But then, the people from the, you know, upper classes—all of them left. Whoever is working right now is being compensated."

"So they're being paid wages?"

"They're being given food. That's the . . . compensation . . . "

"So they're working for food, they're not demanding wages?"

"Well, if you think about it, whatever they used to earn when they worked elsewhere—they could barely manage a square meal with those wages, nothing else. So . . . " The man seemed a little embarrassed.

Shahed's eyes wandered back to the young woman's breasts.

"What a mess! Why don't you get out of here?" Shahed mumbled under his breath.

Then he shut his eyes again and tried to focus on the next question. "In that case, they're free to work wherever they want, aren't they?"

The man laughed silently. "Of course! But where's the work, sahib? There's hardly any these days . . . So when they get their meals in exchange for work, they do it gladly."

"There's no work anywhere else—write that down, and have you written about the wageless labour?" Shahed asked Muneer.

Muneer shook his head. Shahed suddenly became furious. He leaned towards Muneer, brought his mouth close to his ears and growled like a caged animal, "Motherfucker! What the fuck have you come here for? Stop fooling around and write."

Shahed sat back on his chair. He simply couldn't remain upright anymore. He said, "So, you're saying that when this canal has been dug, the water will come. But what if it does? What happens then?"

The man's face turned red. Like a teacher explaining to a dunce, he said, "What are you saying, sahib? Don't you realise what will happen when the water comes? The two barren fields on both banks of the river will be fertile once again. We don't get even one crop in the year now. When the water comes, we will have at least two crops a year. We'll have more grain. The scarcity of water in the region . . . "

He would have continued, but Shahed interrupted him with a question in the most indifferent of tones. "These people digging the canal—do all of them own land on the river banks?"

The man kept staring at Shahed with his cold snake-like eyes.

"I'm asking you—the people who are working on the canal right now—how many of them own land on the river banks?"

Unable to dodge the question, the man said, "Almost all of them are poor labourers, sahib. I don't think any of them owns any land anywhere."

"Very well. What about the people who do own the land on the two banks of the river—is any of them digging the canal?"

The man was visibly embarrassed by now. He stammered, "Not exactly digging . . . I mean . . . you see . . . the ones who own la . . . large tracts of land are not here. There are some landowners who are here though—they own small portions of land—who are overseeing the project."

"I'm sure you yourself own some land on the river banks."

"Yes . . . a little . . . "

"So, you must be 'overseeing' too, isn't that so?" Shahed winked at the man. But when the man didn't reply, he became grave once again. He said, "If the canal does bring water to the river, and thanks to the river, if the soil does become fertile, and if it gives a crop, will these men and women own the harvest?" Shahed pointed in the direction of the five hundred and odd men and women toiling away.

"Look sahib, they'll benefit too. Whatever crop is grown will feed them too."

"I see. So, all of you—the owners of the land—will carry the grain to their houses personally?"

The man didn't reply.

Shahed yelled, "Let's talk about you. Will you take your excess crop and distribute it among those men?"

"N-no . . . " The man stammered.

"So? The landowners are using government money to get irrigation for their lands—right? And the people who are actually digging the canal own nothing—neither the land nor the crop. Shut up, Muneer . . . "

Muneer had raised his pen and was about to speak when Shahed reprimanded him sharply.

The beggars had moved away from the tent by now. The young woman had also left. Shahed looked out towards the river through halfclosed eyes. There were innumerable creases on his forehead, under his eyes, on his fleshy chin and on his jaws. They resembled the deep gashes of a knife on the bark of a tree. The loudspeaker continued to blare one song after another. Shahed looked at the blinding sunlight outside, the spades moving up and down rhythmically, white dust rising from the ground, the dark bodies of the labourers bending like sticks of cane and then straightening again, loose earth sliding off their bodies, thin streams of sweat running down their shiny backs like snakes. He felt he was among those men and women now—as if he could hear them clenching their teeth and digging away, moistening the loose earth with their sweat and smearing the mud on their bodies to get some relief from the heat. Shahed realised he was close to dropping off. Rubbing his eyes, he looked at the sky again. It was like a blue bag of gunpowder, hanging heavy, about to explode any time now. He looked at the leaves on the trees and watched them wilt. The din raised by five hundred famished and exhausted men and women seemed to deafen him.

Shahed shook his thoughts off and rose to his feet. "Come Muneer. All right then my friend, carry on with your work."

The man stood up hurriedly and said, "No, no, please don't leave rightaway. I've sent for daab, they'll be here any minute."

"We'll leave them for you. We're late already, we have to go." The moment Shahed and Muneer stepped out of the tent, the beggars surrounded them again. The young woman was there too. Shahed exploded in rage: "Get lost! Get lost, you bastards! He was right—each one of you needs to be shot. Bloody beggars . . . "

It was almost two o'clock by the time they reached the restaurant. Shahed hadn't spoken a single word on the way back. Looking at his rotund companion walk in the intense heat with big frog-like steps, Muneer wondered if he was about to drop dead in the middle of the field.

But Shahed did make it to the hotel. Sitting on a chair, he didn't speak for about ten minutes. But only for ten minutes. And then, his morose expression made way for a smile, followed by good-natured bantering with the young boy who served them. "Ah there you are my dark prince, do bring us something to eat. I told you to cook some chicken for us, I hope it's ready."

Just like he had in the morning, the boy bared his red gums and nodded.

"Excellent! Go bring it. Bring the whole pot. If I find anything missing, I'll kill you. I'm starving."

Shahed gobbled up the food, rinsed his hands and mouth, pulled out a packet of Dunhills from his pocket and extended it to Muneer. "Here." Then he lit one, burnt it almost halfway down with a single drag, looked at Muneer with a smile on his face and said, "Now tell me."

"Tell you what?" asked Muneer.

"Whatever you want to." Shahed glanced in the direction of the station and choked on the smoke from his cigarette. A man was sitting on a small gunny bag at one end of the platform, selling boiled rice by the weight. As he held the scales up, Shahed could see a small mound of white rice on one of the pans. A couple of small black pots were placed near him. Perhaps they contained curry. There was no dearth of customers. The rice was selling well. Two or three men were staring at the uncovered pot of rice with greedy eyes, but were hesitant about approaching it.

"What the hell is going on?" Shahed asked, staring.

"He's selling rice," replied Muneer.

"Thank you, idiot, I can see that! But why the hell is he selling rice?"

"Shahed Bhai, I've noticed you becoming sentimental quite often. You just paid for your meal, didn't you? Why are you shocked to see a man selling rice on the platform?"

"Have you ever seen anyone weighing cooked rice on a scale and selling it openly? Anywhere in Bangladesh? A hundred grams of rice, a quarter kilo of rice—what rubbish!"

"But even restaurants sell it that way, don't they?"

"Stop blabbering like a silly woman, Muneer. I'll slap the hell out of that stupid head of yours. Restaurants! Is it the same as selling rice by the weight on an open platform?"

"Why, they've been selling roti-subzi on platforms for a long time now."

"Again you're talking nonsense. Are rice and roti-subzi the same?"

Muneer decided against responding. The vendor's arm was still up in the air, holding the scales. The sun's rays had begun to soften a bit. The man was sitting in the shade under a huge rain tree on the platform. A bare-bodied boy of seven or eight with a protruding belly had been sitting in front of the pot of rice for a long time now. Suddenly he grabbed a fistful from the pot and stuffed it in its mouth. The vendor didn't waste a single moment. Putting the scales down, he punched the boy hard on his back. Several grains of rice shot out of the boy's mouth like a dozen white insects and fell on the platform. He writhed in pain, gasping for air, a lump of rice blocking his throat.

"He's going to choke to death . . . choke to death . . . " Shahed threw his cigarette away and stood up in excitement.

But the boy had recovered by then. The vendor was back to weighing out his rice, unperturbed. Muneer had sunk back in his chair. He could see only the vendor's dark arm rising with the scales. If a customer tried to put some extra rice on the pan, the vendor's left rose mechanically and pushed the customer's hand away. That's all Muneer could see. Shahed leaned back against the wooden wall of the room, lit another cigarette and said, "Have you written about the revolution?"

"What revolution?" Muneer's voice held a note of caution.

"This one—I'm talking about the canal."

"But Shahed Bhai, there's one thing you haven't considered'—Muneer spoke with confidence—'It is true that those poor landless villagers are selling their labour cheaply. It is also true that more than half the people living in Bangladesh don't own any land. Therefore, if the canal can be dug successfully, then it would benefit only the landowners, and not the ones who dug it. All of this is true. But what about productivity? Don't you think agricultural productivity will increase? Take paddy for example—if the total yield increases because of the canal, then the poor villagers will benefit too, correct? The government will not have to import foodgrains."

Shahed answered calmly, "But explain this to me—how will the crop get to the poor workers? It's true that the price of paddy will drop if output increases. But what about the wages of these labourers? Will they remain the same?"

"No," said Muneer, "They will drop."

"As you can see, in no circumstances do the people belonging to this class benefit much—their situation, their position, their problems . . . everything remains unchanged. Their purchasing power will never increase. It's all pre-arranged, my friend, it's all pre-arranged. Mark my words. If a group of people get together and do something which improves the economy, there will always be people to negate it and balance things out. There are black-marketers, there are people who supply bonded labour . . . " Shahed seemed eager to present a hundred other arguments to Muneer. "You won't understand, I don't understand all of it either. And then there's capitalism. There too, the entire focus is on increasing production. Now one word of criticism for capitalism from you and I'll blow your head off." Shahed broke into loud laughter. "I don't understand all this production business my friend, assholes openly selling cooked rice by the weight . . . wok!"

Shahed's face turned a deep red. The veins on his throat had swollen. Covering his mouth with his hand, he dashed out of the room, ran around the corner and started throwing up.

Muneer continued to smoke without paying any attention to the violent sounds outside. The sun was about to set, the vendor sitting beneath the rain tree was still weighing rice on the platform. Muneer's thoughts turned towards his flat in Dhaka, where his ten-year-old son and eight-year-old daughter were now in the care of a nanny. Their mother had left. She would never come back. The little girl had recently learnt how to tie her hair in plaits. She looked just like her mother. His son was growing unusually tall by the day. He had outgrown his shorts, appearing quite silly in them. Lost in his thoughts, Muneer choked on smoke and flung his cigarette away. As he rose to his feet, Shahed entered, his face and shirt soaked in water. He looked like he was dead twice over.

"Come Shahed Bhai, let's go back to the rest house," Muneer said. "It seems you aren't feeling too well."

"Yes, let's go." Shahed stepped towards the door.

"Shall I help you? Can you walk?"

"You don't have to help me. Try to find a rickshaw."

They were about to step out of the hotel when the young woman with the baby appeared before them. Managing to avoid a collision, Muneer turned to stare at her. She was standing a couple of feet away, her slightly longish and full breasts hanging out. A few scrawny strands of hair were stuck to her mouth and face, which were under a layer of dust and sand. It seemed to Muneer that wiping her face with a wet handkerchief would make it glow. He threw a quick glance at Shahed. The young woman sighed heavily—the lack of foul odour in her breath seemed quite curious.

The two men walked away from the restaurant quickly. When they reached the rest house, Shahed threw himself on the wicker chair without changing out of his dirty clothes or taking a wash and said, "Get it out, it's in my suitcase."

"What is?" Muneer was confused.

"Open the suitcase and see. It's unlocked. There must be a little left."

Muneer realised what Shahed was talking about. "Oh, you brought it along with you? But you don't seem to be feeling well. Are you sure you want to drink now?"

"I'm not going to drink it all by myself you idiot. You'll drink with me. It's good, the quality is amazing. Come on, come on, get it out."

Muneer opened the suitcase and brought out the bottle of whisky, looking at the bottle appreciatively. "But you almost puked your guts out. Are you going to drink on an empty stomach?"

"Yes sir, you don't have to worry about that. No, no! No water."

The sun had set by then, but there was still a faint light. Muneer switched on the light. A soft cool breeze was blowing outside. The light inside the room seemed unusually bright. Muneer threw a piercing glance at Shahed. After one or two sips, Shahed's face began to show some colour. Muneer noticed the beads of perspiration gathering on Shahed's forehead and flowing down the crevices of his cheeks. It seemed to him that, just like overripe apples and pears in the market, parts of Shahed's face had also started to rot.

Shahed yelled, "Did you see the confidence with which that man was speaking today? The swine's hired beggars and daily labourers to dig the canal—the bastard! You! Are you even listening?"

"Hmm?" Muneer was lost in his thoughts. Shahed's loud, intoxicated voice startled him.

"What the hell are you thinking about, huh? Here I am blabbering away, and you . . . tell me something—where has the nation planted its feet? You have to tell me, you son of a bitch!"

"On the breast of the poor," Muneer replied unexpectedly.

"What did you say? What did you say? On the breast of the poor? Bugger, now you are talking sense!" Shahed laughed out loud. "Well said, well said, on the breast of the poor!"

Muneer was now quite worried. He had no intention of spending the entire night with a drunk companion. And it seemed the man had decided to drink till he passed out! Suddenly, Shahed brought his face close to Muneer's, so close that Muneer could see the pores in his skin. The strong smell of whisky filled Muneer's nostrils as Shahed said gravely, "Don't be silly! Don't make the stupid and baseless assumption that I'm drunk. But yes, I tell you the truth—I'm very disturbed, I've been disturbed the entire day. This is a strange country—the fucker was sitting in the open and selling cooked rice on the road. And . . . and that kid . . . crying with his mouth open, choking on the rice—fuck! Bloody hell . . . "

Muneer said, "Really Shahed Bhai, you're not feeling too well tonight. Come on, I'll put you to bed."

With a fuddled smile Shahed said, "No, believe me. This isn't enough whisky to get me drunk. No, it's not that. Fuck, if only we could get a woman in here."

"What?" Muneer was obviously not amused. "What nonsense, Shahed Bhai!"

"Nonsense? What's so nonsensical about it? A woman is a woman, that's all!"

Muneer smiled. "Are you serious? You want me to get one for you? You don't know me—if I step out that door, I'll come back with a woman."

"A-ha! Don't think I don't know you! You swine!" Shahed laughed "But who do you think you're trying to scare, eh? Do you know how many years it has been since my wife died? I've got two kids, both boys—I haven't seen them in ages. They don't call, they don't write. I'm practically dead to them. Why do they care if I get a woman in here? Why does anyone care? Do you think I'm a human being? No—I'm a gentleman! Which is another way of saying everything about me is fake! I'm fake, and my profession is all about faking. I'm faking the truth under the guise of journalism—day after day after day. Listen, if the people of this country strip me naked, make me stand in the middle of the city and kick me in my ass, do I have anything to complain about? No sir! Not a thing! Because I deserve it. So therefore, my friend, I'm not afraid, I don't give a fuck. Let's see how big a hero you are—please go and get a whore in here."

A soft rustle made Muneer turn around. The young woman, without the child with her now, was standing in the doorway, her palm resting softly on the wooden frame, a beautiful, dazzling smile floating on her lips, her breasts still hanging out.

Like a wounded beast, Shahed let out an insane death scream that shook the foundations of the entire building. "Send her away, send her away, for heaven's sake, send her away . . . "

IN
SEARCH
OF
HAPPINESS

"How cool the shade over there must be! It's calling out to me."
Kunkum had stuffed the pillow between her chest and the bed
and was staring beyond the well in the backyard. As the screech
of the afternoon tore through the skies, a grey crow flew down
from its perch and took shelter under the shaddock tree. Kunkum
watched as it bathed in the puddle—how happy it looked as it
dipped its throat in the dirty water, wet its wings and sat under
the tree scratching its head with its claws! And then the pain
started. Kunkum was torn apart. Into countless bits and pieces.
As if someone was wailing her heart out. As if someone had seen
the signs of happiness on a brand new currency note and had
turned it around to come face to face with sorrow itself. With
such strange thoughts going through her head, Kunkum felt like
taking a walk down the corridors of her memory. Just like
rummaging through a box of old letters. She felt happiness
breathing on her skin, an unusual sensation—the kind of feeling
you get on touching some forgotten and once-loved piece of
attire, or when you caress your dead mother's pretty jewels.

How strange! She thought to herself. *I felt as if I was drowning in an ocean of grief. But there was no ocean when I opened my eyes and looked for it.*

Kunkum dragged herself out of the bed and stepped up to the window. There it was, the afternoon—stagnant, still. A dove called out from the branches of a mango tree towards the south. Kunkum rested her chin on a bar of the window grill and gazed outside for a while. But the afternoon didn't move an inch, hanging from the sky, motionless and still. As the minutes went by, twenty-two-year-old Kunkum grew tired of watching and judging herself, becoming quite irritated. Because she hardly seemed to be able to hold on to anything in life. Neither grief, nor joy. Or perhaps they only came and left in a hurry. She reached out for them. But it felt miserable. The pain, that awful pain, rose from within. Her breast felt empty, hollow. Her head hurt so bad that she had to lie down, and that too at the oddest of hours. Gradually she lost her consciousness. When the trouble first began, a distinct and genuine frown had appeared on Rajeeb's fair forehead. He had drawn Kunkum to his breast in a bid to comfort her. "Hysteria? Of all things?"

Kunkum had said wearily, "I wonder what's wrong with me. I've never had this problem before. I did use to have severe headaches as a little girl, but it helped when I started wearing glasses. And then in college, the headaches were back. I remember once I dropped a pebble into a dark and dry well. I heard the soft sound of the pebble hitting the bottom. Ever since then, I often have a strange empty feeling inside."

"These are simply your obsessions. Women are known to have chronic psychological problems. But aren't these problems supposed to get corrected after marriage?" The conviction with which Rajeeb had spoken had been enough to make Kunkum feel guilty and answerable.

"Anyway, there's nothing to worry. It'll get better on its own." Had it been such assurances made by Rajeeb that had brought on the symptoms more regularly? Because, soon afterwards, the problem began to recur at certain precise hours. Take the afternoon when Rajeeb had come home from work earlier than usual, producing a maroon sari from the packet in his hand while he deliberately surveyed her dazzling, immaculate body. Spotting the greed in his eyes, Kunkum had put up an act—as though she were bubbling with joy within, as if she had not had a splitting headache since that morning. But as she had put on the new sari and was waiting like an empress in her bedchamber, her head started hurting so much that she lost her senses, leaving the helpless man with no other option but to sacrifice all his plans of soft seduction and resort to unthinkable acts of sheer barbarism. The man who had always been in the habit of coming home straight from work, the man who would often drop everything and rush home to shower his passionate love upon her, no longer came home before eleven o'clock.

The light of the sun was dying, the evening had begun to descend upon the terrace. But this privacy, this solitude—hadn't they agreed to share this?

"This is why I didn't want to take a house in the city, you know." Rajeeb had smiled. "How would I have cuddled you otherwise?"

And then a beautiful bed, steel almirah, dressing table, bookrack—and many other pieces of furniture straight from

Kunkum's dreams had been procured, and a sweet little plan of living a beautiful life, capitalising on the combined youth of twenty-two springs on one side of the bed and twenty-seven on the other, was drawn up and executed; but the grand weariness of lifelong companionship soon began to eat into any and all notions of marital bliss, like dust that gets into old boxes and trunks, like insects that infiltrate tins of rice and jars of biscuits, eating into them bit by bit.

"You have to tell me clearly what your problem is, what's bothering you," Rajeeb had said. Kunkum could only refer to the darkness of the well, and that too in a distant, far-away voice. As a result, Rajeeb didn't come home before eleven o'clock anymore.

As she stood by the window, these were the thoughts that were going through Kunkum's mind. The slanting rays of the sun were kissing her forehead.

"I have to make an effort to dismiss all negative thoughts. Or else I'll go mad," muttered Kunkum under her breath, picking up her sari, petticoat, blouse, and soap and walking out towards the well. A heavy silence seemed to hang over the area. Kunkum stepped up to the shaddock tree. The area under the thickest network of branches was deep in the shade now, while there was a constant play of shadow and light where the branches were as sparse as hair on a balding pate. Draping her sari and other things over the bamboo fence, Kunkum peered into the well. As she gazed at the cold dark water, a shiver ran through her. As though her entire body had suddenly turned thirsty. And then, as she locked the small door, she felt very lonely. Usually it was during these moments, when she took off her blouse and the brassiere within, that she felt the world around her come alive. The solitary crow cawed, a little shriller this time. A dove cooed. A dry leaf floated from a tree to the ground. The wind whistled through the trees. And yet, despite all these sounds, she felt a sense of calmness. Although she knew that hundreds of living creatures of the natural world could now see her in the nude, she felt no shyness. Kunkum picked a centipede up from the ground and placed it on her palm, dropping a few drops of water to create a small puddle in its path. She watched a dragonfly rub its head with its leg. She stood as motionless as a block of stone to ensure that a butterfly perched on her hair didn't fly away. One could say that she opened herself up to the mute world, finding bliss in letting go.

After the bath, Kunkum returned to the bedroom and was surprised to see Rajeeb lying on the bed with his hand over his eyes. His fair forehead and pointed nose were peeping out of from behind his fingers. He had not taken off his clothes—not even his shoes. The sight reminded Kunkum of the day of her wedding. Seeing him for the first time had made Kunkum feel as though she had been married to a prince after all, just like in the books. Her mind had not been able to absorb the fact that that handsome man was now hers forever.

"Are you all right? Why are you home at this hour?"

Rajeeb simply glanced at her in response. Had this happened a couple of months ago, Kunkum would have found herself in seventh heaven. And Rajeeb too would not have waited for questions—he would have said, "Didn't feel like being in office today. So, I came home. Truth is, I wanted to see you."

But no, there he was, lying silent in bed. A splitting headache, possibly.

Slashing her sheathe of happiness, Kunkum returned to reality. "Do you have a headache?" she asked.

"Yes."

"Then why did you go out into the sun? You could have waited for some time," Kunkum said, her eyes turning sad.

Rajeeb was looking at her sternly. "You haven't had lunch yet?"

"I'll have it now."

"What were you doing all this while? I went to work at ten. It's half past three now. You're still lazing?" Rajeeb sounded as though his headache had suddenly vanished, and that he had come home at this odd hour with the sole objective of admonishing his wife. Kunkum was at a loss for words. Did he think she had whiled away her time and had starved all day only to prove her apathy towards Rajeeb?

I have never understood myself fully, Kunkum thought as she walked into the kitchen and started pouring cold lumps of rice and curry down her throat. *When I was a little girl, when I used to wear a frock, when I used to run after butterflies, when I used to recite poetry loudly, I never knew what happiness was although I was happy. Oh, how happy I was! How strong, how warm that feeling of happiness was!*

Kunkum stared out of the window and saw a little bird jumping around on the branch of the custard-apple tree. When you were happy, you didn't know it. Because the moment you became conscious of your happiness, it vanished into thin air. Time—the present moment, that is—entered the very pores of everything that made you happy and tore them apart with its fangs.

But unlike the present, the past lovingly threw a comforting sheath of nostalgia over everything. Kunkum realised her mind was beginning to wander. So she tried to get a grip and arrange her thoughts in order. *When I grew up, I learnt how to dream. And what a surprise—all my dreams have come true! Rajeeb. A life of comfort. I have everything that I had ever dreamt of adorning my bedroom with—except the almirah, of course, which was not made of teak. And oh yes, the clothes-stand, which was decidedly cheap and tasteless. But still, one could say all my dreams have come true. And yet, I was happier when I was dreaming than when those dreams did come true.*

The sun wasn't strong any more by the time Kunkum stepped out of the kitchen. Standing in the middle of the yard, she looked up at the sky, which looked almost white, with birds flying across its expanse.

A most beautiful evening was coming down from the sky, she mused. *If there's anything in this world that can make me happy, it is when I gaze at a sky like this, when I watch those squirrels frolicking in the branches of the tree, when the vast sky and nature herself look down at my nude body in mute witness, when a hum begins to sound from the heart of the earth—I like it very much then, and I think this is what happiness is, and that I can forever, forever be happy.*

Ending this chain of thought, she turned around to enter her cavern of sorrow again, climbing two steps to the veranda. Suddenly Kunkum saw a large lizard on the wall, waiting motionlessly as it watched an insect. She stopped abruptly, a searing pain rising from her chest, manifesting itself in the form of droplets of sweat like sweat on her chin, lips and forehead. The lizard's body undulated from its neck, along its back, all the way to the tail as it crept closer to the insect without a sound. It was now next to its prey, lying in wait, watching the quarry with cold brass-coloured eyes. Kunkum turned around in horror to find nature waiting with bated breath. When the lizard pounced, she gave up, rushing into the room with a muted cry of pain.

Rajeeb had sat up on the bed by now, staring at her. Kunkum clutched the backrest of the chair, placing her hand on the flat of the table and caressing the bookrack. She moved about the room, pleading in her head for protection from all the things that she had ever dreamed of adorning the room with. And amidst the crowd of all the furniture damaged by the fangs of time, amidst the tarnished household items doomed by the day-to-day struggle of a nondescript life, as a dazed Rajeeb now grabbed her and stared into her eyes—the woman found herself drowning in the tides of sorrow rising from the very depths of her own existence. And all she could see around herself was a dense darkness.

WITHOUT
NAME
OR
LINEAGE

He came by the evening train. Winter had just begun to set in. He was wearing a thick, rough tweed coat. The fox-grey colour went well with his bronzed complexion. An old yet expensive tie hung loosely around his neck. His trousers had faded—the thighs highlighted by two or three thick stitches. He came by the evening train.

Dusk was falling. He stared at the southern end of the platform absentmindedly. The shadows were moving away quickly. As the red-tinged sunshine began to disappear behind the tall buildings and treetops towards the west, a wintry darkness descended.

The man now stared at the dust-ridden road leading away from the station towards the west. The surface had worn away, and was covered with white dust. The road was lined on both sides with tin sheds, now standing empty. The sheds were separated by dark alleys between them. There was not a soul to be seen.

The engines were shunted with a hissing sound. The man had the distinct feeling that they were running on their own in this godforsaken place. It seemed to him that they neither had any specific destination nor any urgency to go anywhere. The low-roofed houses on the eastern side of the station, were quickly sinking into the darkness—their brick chimneys now a faded outline against the sky.

The man walked out of the station unmindfully, the leather folio bag in his hand swinging. He hadn't seen a single man or woman so far on the platform or within the station. But as he was stepping out through the gate, he noticed a few soldiers huddled inside a small room next to it. They were having a chat, their rifles on their knees. Their helmets were pulled low over their brows. They looked at him with cold eyes, but didn't say anything, continuing to talk amongst themselves coarsely. As he passed through the gate hurriedly, one of the soldiers raised his rifle and pointed it at him.

"No, no—not now." Another soldier lowered the rifle gently. The first soldier grinned foolishly. Passing through the gate, the man found himself in a circular yard. There was nothing in the middle except some grass covered in dust. He began walking, his shoes working up a rhythm on the paved road. He moved along the edge of the circular yard—no one anywhere. Pausing, he looked at the other roads connecting the station with various parts of the town. Some were laid with stone chips—others were paved but riddled with dusty potholes. The road that led to the village was unpaved, however. There were no buildings on either side.

The man entered a restaurant nearby—the one with the tin walls. He was quite hungry. It was chilly inside, and the solitary bulb that was burning was enveloped in thick smoke. All he could see in the dim light were the dirty tables and chairs in the dingy room. The place had seemed empty and abandoned at first. But soon he could make out a man sitting at a counter near the door, resting his chin on his palm, and another by the fire in the clay oven. As the man at the counter looked up at him, he rubbed the stubble on his cheek and asked mildly, "Can I get something to eat here?"

"No," came the brief, irritated response.

"No food? Nothing at all?"

"No, nothing." The other man waved his hand as if to shoo away an invisible fly.

"Perhaps a cup of tea?" The traveller asked, fingering the patches on his tweed coat.

"There's nothing here. Get lost!"

As he left he felt the other man watching him, staring at his broad shoulders from the back. He found himself in total darkness outside, with no lights on the road. He walked along the big wide street, his steps muffled by the thick layer of dust. As far as he could remember, this road had never been so barren and devoid of trees. There used to be a signboard-painting shop right here. Over there, a homoeopath used to see his patients. Bright lights would shine in the evenings. A shrivelled old doctor used to sit in a pharmacy on the other side of the road. A couple would occupy a bench in front of a shop and peer at their newspapers over the thick frames of their glasses. He tried to remember why he was here. Perhaps he owed someone money, or maybe he was to receive something from someone else—he really wasn't sure.

Tiny bits and pieces of memory sparked inside his head—for instance, waking up in the morning and shaving, or reading the newspaper. He recalled crying on reading about Patrice Lumumba's death. One afternoon—yes, it was an afternoon, he faintly remembered—when he had read Ho Chi Minh's poetry. As the sweet chimes of bells came floating from the hills—ding ding ding—well-endowed young girls pranced swiftly down to the valley. He recollected, as a child, digging underground for large round potatoes.

No one came, he saw no one around him. Turning left, he walked into a dark alleyway between the tin sheds. It seemed to him that the grass here had not been trod on for some time. His feet sank into the soft earth. He touched the tin wall of the sheds and found them wet with dewdrops, and ice-cold. Walking on, he finally reached the river bank. He recognised the place—this was the market. A number of shops lined the road. But they were all shut.

The road was nothing but the paved bank of the river, with shops on both sides. The shops on the side of the river had no ground beneath them—the river had washed it all away. All of them hung in the air, raised above the water on thick bamboo stalks or tree trunks. He could hear the soft lapping of the waves as they hit the shore in the dark. It seemed to him that the ground beneath his feet had also become hollow, and that the water had seeped beneath the spot where he now stood. Through gaps between the shops on his left he saw the river—a vast dense chunk of darkness—flowing along silently. A few flickering specks of light signalled the presence of boats and a thick curtain of fog.

Threatened by the river, this road had been paved with black cobblestones in the distant past. The stones now protruded out of the surface here and there; some of them had even come loose. The man stumbled in the dark once or twice. But he didn't care. He was in an ever-increasing state of shock. There was not a single human being around. No one came up to him and spoke. There was no lamp or lantern anywhere. The doors of the houses were sealed shut, like jaws clamped tight after seeing a horrible sight. He felt a sudden urge to insert a metal spoon between the two rows of teeth to pry the jaws open. Stirred by curiosity, he stepped up on the low veranda of one of the houses and tried to peep inside. His eyes met nothing but total blackness. He tried to push the door open a crack, but the heavy door didn't move an inch. A sudden and strong whiff of red-chillies hit his nose. He turned around to leave and tripped on a black goat in the darkness, falling heavily on the ground with a loud thud.

For the first time he heard the sound of heavy boots. Several of them. Coming up from the depths of the darkness—like the clip-clop of a horse. And then a loud, unfamiliar voice pierced the silence.

"Who's there?"

Before the sound could fade away, he heard the crack of a rifle shot. The sound of the boots was now moving away—in a different direction. One more shot rang out. The man got to his feet slowly, clutching his folio bag to his chest. He waited for a minute or two before resuming his journey cautiously. He negotiated the intricate labyrinth of dark lanes, ghostly shops and deserted roads—much like a centipede crawls through a maze.

After some time, he reached the central square of the town and passed the wide streets in succession. These areas too were steeped in darkness. Then he started making his way up a spiral staircase. There was a faint light all around, although he couldn't locate the source. He stared at the wall—the plaster had peeled off at places. A damp rank smell choked him, making him gasp. The stairs seemed like an ancient tunnel. A soft breeze was blowing. He began to tremble from head to toe. As he grabbed the rough wall for support, a cold tremor began to creep up his fingers. There was a pencil sketch of a woman's face on the wall, and, right next to it, a couple of exposed bricks jutted out in sheer irony. Where was the light coming from? He began to go up the floors—first floor, second, and then the third. At the end of the stairs, he banged on the door and yelled.

"Asit? Are you there? Are you home, Asit?"

The banging seemed to shake the house to its core. The very foundations began rumbling, as in an earthquake. The man continued to pound on the door with his fists.

"Asit? Where are you? Are you in there?"

A soft sound was heard from the other side of the door. The frightened voice of a young girl was heard.

"Who's there? Who's outside?"

But the man continued to yell Asit, Asit, without paying heed to anything else. He stopped only when one of the doors parted a little. The pale, thin face of a woman peeped out. The fear writ large on her face embarrassed him. Her eyes looked like they would pop out any second. She was holding on to the door for dear life.

"What do you want?"

"Is Asit home? This is Asit's home, isn't it?"

"No, there's no one here by that name. Who are you?"

"But . . . do you know if someone with that name used to live here?"

"I don't know. We're new to this town." The woman banged the door shut. The light seemed to go out suddenly. The man stood in the cold at the end of the stairs. Supporting himself against the banister, he stared down the flight of stairs—a deep pit of darkness—and prepared himself for the jump. Then he tried to leap into the darkness, just like a cat on a bale of cotton. But moments later he found himself climbing down the stairs—his shoes striking the steps loudly and the sound echoing within the deserted tunnel. It took a long time to make his way down. He stepped outside once again, and sat down on a cold culvert, with his knees drawn up to his chin.

There was a rifle shot in the distance. The wind had stopped blowing, and it was a cloudless, starless sky. He waited for something, perhaps a horrible shriek to pierce through the black sheathe of the night. But nothing happened, and, fed up of waiting, he started walking again. The houses on either side of the road resembled boxes. The low roofs shone in the dark. Paved roads and dusty alleys ran between them, straight into the heart of terror.

He heard the rattle of a heavy vehicle behind him, although he wasn't sure of the source of the sound. It was constant, but its intensity varied. The vehicle seemed to be twisting and turning through a serpentine road—alternately moving away and coming closer. He felt irritated again.

It was quite cold. He pulled up the collar of his coat as much as possible and tried to cover his ears, rubbing his palms together. The houses stood in deathly silence, their doors tightly shut. Not a streak of light was to be seen anywhere, no spoken word to be heard.

As he turned right into an alley, a jeep screeched into a sudden halt in the distance. He heard the faint groan of a female voice. An overwhelming sense of despair turned him hollow inside. An earthen wall had once collapsed on him, smothering him and making it impossible to breathe. He felt that way tonight. He started walking towards the jeep—wondering if this was all a dream within a dream, or if it was indeed happening. With the sudden strike of a match, a small flash of flame lit up the cruel face of a foreigner, along with a woman's—gagged and bound. As he approached the vehicle, someone jumped in and it sped away into the dark.

Looking up at the sky, the man was surprised to see that the moon had come up. He was now standing on the corner of the widest road in town. The moon was climbing quickly, and he could see all the way to the end of the road. The houses resembled a row of ancient abandoned buildings in the middle of a desert. As though they had only just been excavated, standing and proudly narrating the untold story of a town long dead. The whitewashed structures shone in the moonlight. Each of them cast its own shadow on the road or on the building next to it. Some of the houses had low walls running around them. On the other side of the walls, he could see flower-plants, overgrown weeds and vines, mossy bricks. Some had signs on their gates— 'Beware of the Dog'—although no barking could be heard. Some were big, and others, small and modest. Some were new and recently painted, some were old and damp. A few open spaces were visible, some haphazardly located alleys. And it was through these alleys between buildings that he kept walking—with his erect frame, in his tweed coat and dusty boots. He walked like a machine. His pace was neither fast nor slow. It could perhaps be best described as relentless, uninterrupted, like the ticking of a clock. But soon he stopped walking and sat down in the middle of the road, taking off his shoes and then his socks.

"Aaah!" An exclamation of pleasure escaped his lips as his feet became free. He shook the dust out of his socks and knocked the sole of his boots on the road to clear out the pebbles. Then he stood up once again, shoes and socks in hand, and continued to walk barefoot along the alley.

Halfway through, he heard footsteps and voices from the main road ahead.

"Don't lie, you son of a bitch! Are you from the Joy Bangla brigade?"

"No," came the reply.

"Yes, you are!" The sound of a dull blow came in on the wind. With a strange feeling in his heart, the man went down on all fours and crawled warily towards the main road. Several men were visible in the moonlight.

"You're a Hindu, aren't you?"

"No."

"Of course you are!"

He saw a man—in nothing but a pair of black shorts—surrounded by nine or ten soldiers.

"Where do you live?"

The naked man didn't reply.

"Where's the rest of your gang?"

The man didn't reply.

One of the soldiers stepped forward and punched the naked man heavily across the face. He collapsed on the road, face-forward.

"I'll shoot you down, you bastard."

"Do it now," the man said, wiping the blood off his lips and sitting upright.

"You are with the Mukti Fauj, aren't you, you Bengali pig? Fucking Mujib's dog!"

"No."

"You're not a Hindu?"

"No."

"That's it," the soldier said. "Shoot him now."

"No," said another. "I won't shoot him. Watch what I do instead."

After a few minutes, the man on all fours saw a naked body being hoisted towards the roof of a nearby single-storied building. He was upside down, his head pointing to the ground. His feet were tied to the end of a rope, and a few soldiers were pulling on the other end of the rope from the roof, like drawing water from a well. When the naked man's head was about five feet above the ground, a voice was heard.

"That's it, that's enough. So, tell me now—are you from Joy Bangla or not?"

"No."

"Very well, let him go."

The man's head, with the weight of his entire body behind him, hurtled through the air and was smashed on the paved road below with a thud. A soft groan escaped his lips.

His body began to be hoisted again.

"Let's try again—you are from Joy Bangla, aren't you?"

An unintelligible rasp emerged from the man's throat. With all his strength, he said, "Your time is up. If you don't want to die, leave our country now."

Before he could finish, his head came crashing down on the ground again, making a horrible squishing sound this time.

The man on all fours rose to his feet and staggered out of the alley into a dark bylane. Swaying and reeling like a drunkard, he pushed through the darkness—one alley after another—finally stopping in front of a small single storey house. A small yard, surrounded by a low wall, a lotus in one corner. He walked up to the wide red-tiled veranda, stopped in front of the locked door and called out softly.

"Mamata?"

There was no response. The man called out her name again and again. When he knocked on the door softly, it parted a little. It was pitch dark inside. He stepped into the room and asked, "Mamata? Where are you, Mamata?" He called out to his young son Shovon as well. He came out of the room and walked into the corridor inside the house—there was no one there either. He went into the two rooms on the other side, checked the kitchen and the bathroom. He stumbled in the dark, tripped several times, hurting his feet, but he continued to call out, "Mamata? Mamata?"

Then he stepped into the courtyard inside and looked at the house. All the other buildings in the neighbourhood were tall, and he felt he was looking up from the bottom of a well. Three-quarters of the courtyard was steeped in the dense darkness. There were dry leaves everywhere, crumbling under his feet. Sinking his feet into the layers of dry leaves and walking up to the dead tree, he even peeped into the well. And then he banged his knee against an old rusty spade.

He dropped the shoes and socks, and flung the folio bag away. He took off his coat, tie, and shirt one by one. His hairy chest rose and fell as he breathed heavily. His slightly eccentric expression seemed almost insane now. Picking up the spade in his strong hands, he started digging in the middle of the court-yard. After some time, he stooped to pick up a bone from the ribcage. The bone was curved, like a sword. He brought the it close to his nose and sniffed, caressed it lovingly with his fingers. Then he started digging again. One by one, a wrist bone, a long shinbone, and the bones from a pair of shrivelled, milky white feet came up.

The man dug away furiously. Every now and then, he threw the spade on the ground and knelt and clawed at the loose earth with his fingers like a wild animal. He was sweating profusely—he could taste his salty perspiration on his lips. Finally he found the bone from a little arm. Extracting it, he said, "There you are, Shovon. Good boy."

Then came a long lock of hair, the soft bones of the throat, a little ribcage, a wide hipbone—and, finally, a skull. He held the skull in his hands and stared into the darkness of the empty eye-sockets. Leaning over it, he touched its forehead and brushed the dirt off the grinning rows of teeth.

"Mamata!" The man whispered.

Then he clenched his teeth and put the skull on the ground next to him. With renewed vigour, he picked up the spade and swung away at the ground furiously—he wanted to dig out the heart of the earth from its depths.

THE
PUBLIC
SERVANT

The third day of February was an auspicious day in the life of Mamun Rasheed. At least, that was the case till the third day of February in 1983. Even on the morning of that day in '83, there was no reason for him to doubt it. According to Mamun's calculations, it was on that day that he completed twenty years of his career and eighteen years of married life, and it was on that day that his only son turned sixteen. Unfortunately, Mamun didn't know his own date of birth, but he was convinced that he was born on the third day of February in some unknown year. With so many February thirds bringing good news to him throughout his life, it was quite natural for him to have arrived as a precious gift to this glorious land of Bangladesh on February third. But it was impossible to verify this because his father had never been able to pinpoint the date, resorting to suspicious guesswork like "could have been January or February" or "perhaps it was March" and so on. While the gentleman had meticulously written down the dates and times of birth of all his other children, it was only in Mamun's case that he hadn't bothered. Mamun's siblings had been abject failures in life, at least when compared to him. And this would lead one to believe that man is largely ignorant about the future. When Mamun Rasheed was born, his father was fifty and had already had as many as five children before him.

The sky hung particularly low today, as if it was leaning to observe something keenly on Mamun's terrace. It had taken on the dirty ashen colour of lead, and there had not been a trace of sunlight since morning. A strong chilly wind was blowing—it would start raining soon. The weight of the sky bore down even on the interiors of the house. Mamun had not been going to work for a few days, since he was on long leave. He was dressed in a thick cotton panjabi over a spotless white pyjama, his body wrapped in an old Kashmiri shawl. His drawing room looked like a showroom, with a wall-to-wall carpet—not one from our local Amin Brothers, mind you, but an authentic Iranian piece—a foam-core double sofa settee, a low table, a teapot, a vase, flowers, a bookcase, a couple of bronze nudes, a discus-throwing athlete, and a Zainul, a Sultan, an Aminul Islam, a Qayuum Chowdhury, and a Rafiq-un-Nabi hanging from the walls. In other words, a high-volume den of art! It could be called a melting pot of world culture. Even such a large room was now falling short of space. One of the reasons for which was the lack of peaceful coexistence among these myriad cultural pieces. The climate was one of bitter animosity throughout the day. To the left, for instance, was a piece of Chinese pottery, and right next to it stood a symbol of Bengali heritage, baring its teeth like a mangy dog. On the other side of the room were Matryoshka dolls—symbols of recursion from Russia, a doll within a doll, a moneybag within a money-bag—and, tunnelling past them, world culture had stretched back all the way to Mohenjo-daro. Standing in a corner was a massive wooden elephant from Siam, so huge, in fact, that Mamun's sixteen-year-old son often mounted it to avoid boredom.

This room was now securely locked. First there was the superfine wire mesh door, which was shut. Then came a thick glass door, which was locked too. Then there were the heavy blinds, the colour of molten gold, drawn in a manner that allowed no light to escape into or out of the room. Having closeted himself with such elaborate arrangements, Mamun Rasheed wrapped his Kashmiri shawl tighter and sank his torso deep into his expensive foam-core sofa settee. The shawl was more for decor than for protection, because not the slightest draught could penetrate this fortress of a room. The inside of the room was absolutely silent, like the interior of a grave. Not even the whistling of the roaring winds outside could be heard. But, of course, one could feel its journey towards its unknown destination, thanks to Rabi Thakur's song on the gramophone. There was a music centre against the wall too, in case someone wanted to listen to the crashing of the waves.

Mamun had called his wife thrice since morning. She hadn't come. Mamun was quite tall, and he had had the sofa customised to ensure that it could accommodate his full length, so that he could relax without having to curl his legs. The sofa was quite dear to Mamun's family, for they had seen the world while sitting on it. It was into this sofa that Mamun had sunk himself to taste all the delicious food cooked for him. Even now, he stumbled upon some of those aromas sometimes, and memories hidden in the creases of the sofa. The other day, for instance, he had found a long golden strand of hair. As he pulled it out, he imagined it to be a strand of fine golden fibre between two firm breasts. The hair reminded Mamun of a pair of Atlantic blue eyes. Joanna Hill. Mamun never quite understood why women used perfume. He was of the opinion that a smart man had a keener sense of smell than the most well-bred hunting dog. Oh, the strange fragrances that wafted over this spotless sofa! Quite unnecessary, really. He could clearly tell one woman from another just by her inherent smell, and the use of perfumes only upset this skill.

On the other hand, women had a poor sense of smell. They were also blind, like caterpillars. Their envies and jealousies were centred on themselves. They wanted their men to be wrapped around their waists. Mamun could sit and watch the sky change colours all day. A woman couldn't. Bunch of caterpillars! That was the reason he could dare to call his wife to this very sofa every day. But today, she just wouldn't come. She was lying on the bed in the other room, head down, face buried in her palms. Her waist-length hair was spread on the bed like a Japanese fan, with a single silver streak reaching down to her thigh like a slithering snake. Not like a snake exactly, more like a snakeskin. With the hibernation finally over, the dark serpent had shed its dead white skin and vanished in the woods. How old would his wife be now?

As he sat on the sofa smoking his cigar, Mamun Rasheed let his thoughts wander away from his wife's age. The more he thought about things, the more the thought of February the third kept coming back to his head. He had been working for twenty years now. This country had had a different name when he had taken up the job. There were forests all around, habitable land was scarce and often remote, and the population was much lower. Everything was different those days—rivers and canals, land and water, sunshine and shade. Most of these had turned to grey over the past twenty years. But he couldn't care less. Because, right at the beginning, he had learnt the art of leadership. What a perfect speech he had given that day, with the choicest of words in English! It was quite obvious that day that he had taken great care to learn the language, because it was impossible even for anyone with English as his mother tongue to speak with such fluency. Mamun had noticed that such people always spoke very basic English, and their language had no clarity at all. You couldn't speak in a foreign tongue so eloquently unless allegiance and servitude flowed through your veins. Anyway, it was the core quality of his impeccable use of the language that he rode all the way to the top. You are known as public servants, but in reality, you are the rulers of the public. Therefore do learn how to ride horses and how to wield a whip. For the same reason, learn how to speak in English, because if you speak the language of your countrymen, they will consider you one of their own and piss on your head. We have made all necessary arrangements for you to be separated from those whom you are expected to quell. But you have to play your part as well—so always smile obsequiously, join your palms humbly, and bow and scrape in all modesty to bolster your claim of being a public servant. Or else, these very people will drag you down and skin you alive. After these valuable lessons, Mamun and the rest of the flock in his batch were let loose like a bunch of ducklings into a small pond to hunt for snails and worms. Like everyone else, Mamun too realised one day that the small appendages that had developed under his arm were nothing but wings. And then, on an auspicious day, the entire flock took flight to spread across various parts of the country.

Mamun clearly remembered how his life changed forever thanks to that one spirited speech. Since that day, he had always looked for the highest spot for himself wherever he went—be it a high chair, a stool, or even a small mound on the ground. Mamun had always picked it without any hesitation whatsoever. Even when he reflected on his life, Mamun viewed it as an array of pedestals—ascending step by step until he had reached the vicinity throne at the top. But the throne was like the forbidden fruit—Mamun had never eyed it, nor would he ever try to. The last lesson that he had been taught before taking flight as a full-grown swan was to soar as high as he liked but never to make the mistake of aspiring to that throne. It was strictly forbidden for him—like beef was for Hindus, or pig-blood for Musalmans. The throne was the ultimate seat of power. Although he had been told that he wasn't really a servant of the public but a ruler instead, he was to understand and imbibe the fact that he did have a master—the throne of power. Whom did this power belong to? He was not to question that either. Power had no face.

Really, the first pedestal was high enough. Mamun had raised himself on his toes and tried his best to climb onto it, but it had been just beyond his reach. Finally, he had to draw a stool, stand on it and raise himself to the coveted spot with great effort. That was a long time ago. It had all started on a February third. And it had been all uphill since then. But now one could say he resided among clouds. The bejewelled and decorated throne was within reach—he could even touch it if he wished to. Why, he could even sit on it when no one was around. But Mamun never made that mistake. This blasted place made it impossible to plant your ass on the throne peacefully for more than a few moments. Ass after ass after ass—there were always shiny new faces on that throne. Flowing beard today, clean shaven tomorrow, shiny bald patch today, head full of curly hair tomorrow. Ever changing, ever transient. Mamun never even so much as glanced at the throne. The best one could do in life was to survive. All else could come later. There was no point shooting upwards like a rocket only to crash and break your back. Mamun bit his cigar. The most noteworthy feature of the public was its restlessness. As opposed to the calm serenity of people like him. Power? What power? Had anyone ever heard a paper tiger roar? You want to sit on the throne, suit yourself, but don't expect anything more. Mamun knew where true power really lay. He tore through his cigar with his teeth.

Mamun had learnt to speak very softly. He could speak in three languages—softly, in an unhurried rhythm. It was impossible to predict what word he would utter next, and when he did, it seemed as though there couldn't have been a more apt one. The following were the fundamental aspects of everything that he said. First, any suggestion, any task, whatever it may be, was worthy of his support. Second, any such suggestion or task was also debatable. Third, since the road never ended, only branching out farther and farther into other roads, all that had been said had not really been said. And finally, one could never really look at reality, because reality was unfailingly a picture being painted, a Buddhist construct of sorts.

No matter who ascended to the ultimate throne, the Mamun Rasheeds of the world gathered together in flocks and perched on the branches of power, watching keenly, whispering to one another, their beaks moving, issuing their statements calmly—statements made with words that appeared as black shadows on white newsprint, words that flowed through the veins of the common man like a muddy stream. And there was no one who dared to staunch this flow.

As Mamun stared ahead into the void, he could clearly see his decree taking the form of a current moving steadily towards a human settlement. It could not be stopped. Dams and dykes, boulders and rocks—nothing seemed to be working. Men and women were fleeing home and locking their doors and windows, others were turning around to look the other way, yet others were beating drums and canisters and grimacing and screaming at the top of their voices. And yet, the unstoppable current moved on, razing walls and huts on its way, denuding men and women and children, skinning them alive.

Beads of perspiration began to appear on Mamun's forehead, as often happened when he was inspired. He couldn't sit still any more. He walked up to the corner of the room where the cigar box with intricate wooden designs had been placed. Lifting the lid, he found it empty. Mamun was surprised. The box was full till last night. And he certainly couldn't have smoked all of them by this morning. Had he chewed them off one by one? He stood there for some time, staring blankly. His head felt heavy, so much so that it seemed to droop. A stale sort of smell hit his nostrils. It would be wonderful to peep outside right now, he thought. But how could be achieve this? He would have to walk all the way up to the window. Then he would have to part those impossibly heavy golden blinds. And then those innumerable locks and bolts. Only then would he be able to peep outside and watch the overcast day and see the trees and plants sway in the storm—that too from behind the frosted glass panes.

Mamun turned around. And instantly, his head became clear. He realised he could think clearly again—for instance, about the story of the king and the executioner. The king had wanted his royal artist to paint the severed head of a man. After the artist had finished the painting, the king had not liked it. So he summoned the artist and said—it is obvious that you've never seen a severed human head before. Then he asked his executioner to chop off a slave's head and show it to the artist. There was a difference between a king and an executioner. One could say the king was cruel. But it was difficult to decide whether the executioner was.

The cigars were in the bedroom. A long way from here. Through the door on the western side of the drawing room, past the toilet on the left, past the locked room on the right, and then another locked room on the right, and then a dark passage, followed by a right turn and another long corridor, then a toilet, beyond which lay the bedroom. The entire path was carpeted. Mamun's knees were close to giving way when he finally arrived at the bedroom. He leant against the chest of drawers to support himself. Where were the cigars? Could he ask such a trivial question to the stone statue on the bed? His wife Shayela lay on it, face down. Her feet resembled rose petals. Had the bedclothes not been so impossibly white, the faint tinge of pink on her feet would not have been discernible. And that snake-like silver lining in her cloud of hair.

"Where are the cigars?" Mamun asked very softly.

The end of Shayela's white silk sari fell on the floor silently.

"I want to talk to you about some things." Mamun realised he couldn't keep standing anymore, and sat down on the edge of the bed. The silk was parting. Mamun could now see a portion of his wife's back. He stared at her skin fixedly for some time.

"Can't we at least talk about it?" Mamun said in a soft, calm voice. He knew that once he had convinced Shayela to talk to him, he would have no trouble resolving the issue. Mamun had been able to resolve the most complex of problems innumerable times by simply saying the following words: Let us talk about it. Talk, talk, talk—that's what we want to do—talk! If we talk, we shall overcome all our problems. Man is born with a soft, wet and flat tongue—an organ whose true power he has never been able to realise. It was with that organ that Mamun licked his dry lips now.

"No matter how much we try, it is not always possible to avoid accidents. We have to try to reason with it logically. If you don't do that, the incident will be erased neither from your heart nor from your brain. I think you're being unreasonable in refusing to talk about it. We're going to have to see what we need to do about it."

Mamun realised he had finally talked—yes! He had indeed talked. The words were not falling over each other, they were standing in a row—neatly, in order, forming nooses and traps and patterns of all sorts, a hint of irritation here, a tinge of sarcasm there.

Shayela took her time to sit up. Her thick long locks slid down her waist and fell on the bed. She turned and faced Mamun. Countless tiny wrinkles on her pink lips, a grave face, almost floating in the air, peeping out of a mass of thick dark hair. Shayela stared at Mamun and he looked into her eyes. Not a trace of discomfort in them. And yet a shiver of terror ran down Mamun's spine. He was staring at a thousand-year-old statue, carved out of stone. A cold breeze seemed to lash him. Shayela's lips barely parted and Mamun heard a few words.

"What were you saying?"

Mamun's flat wet soft tongue had turned to stone in his mouth.

"What were you saying, tell me."

"I . . . I want to talk to you."

"Tell me."

"I mean . . . I want to talk about this matter."

"What matter, tell me clearly."

"All I'm saying is that . . . that thing . . . it was an accident."

"What thing was an accident? Don't you know what the thing is called?"

"If we are really going to talk about it, we have to be in the right frame of mind. Right now, you are not. You can't see or hear anything right now."

Having said so much without faltering, Mamun realised he had regained control over his words. He didn't stop. Looking into Shayela's eyes, he said softly, "When do we call something an accident? When an incident causes us great harm—any kind of harm—when we didn't cause the incident, when it was not deliberate, when it was unwanted. That's when we call it an accident. Accidents do not need our permission, nor are we responsible for them. We don't want accidents to take place, but once they have, what option do we have but to accept them?"

"You're calling this an accident?" Shayela looked back at her husband with frightened eyes.

"What else can we call it?"

"Your wife's honour . . . "

"It's not a question of your . . . "

"Yes, you're right. It's not a question of your wife's honour. And that's because your wife's honour is not important to you. I know that very well. Even your own honour is not important to you. I know that you can't be compared to even a filthy millipede or a slithering snake—the people of this country may not know that, but I do. You're like the driver of a dilapidated old cart, whipping your dying horse, and all you can think of is . . . "

"I think we have already established the fact that if we are going to talk about it, then we need to have the patience to both talk and listen. Both! All you are doing right now is ranting. Let me ask you this. Let's say a robber breaks into a house on a lonely afternoon and takes away everything—gold, jewellery, money— even the honour of the lady of the house. Tell me, what on earth can the lady do? No matter what she does, is there any way to bring back her honour?"

Shayela's face turned as white as paper. Her eyes looked ready to pop out of their sockets, the white becoming visible, as if she was looking at a giant monster.

"Why have you come to talk to me? What are you trying to explain to me? Do you think I don't know what you look like under that skin of yours? Do you think I have never seen your filthy ugly face? No matter how much you cover up, I can still see right through you."

"I don't cover up anything, I've never hidden anything, at least from you. It's not like we were married yesterday. We've spent a long time together. And we've never had any secrets from each other, Shayela."

A lovely head began to shake on a conch-white neck. A slightly sharp set of teeth, as if filed with a rasp, peeped through the beautifully curved lips. A strange smile appeared on Shayela's face.

"You're right, there are no secrets between us any more. We stand naked, completely naked, we've been stripped bare. I knew this day would come."

"I don't know what is it that you're trying to say. There's been only one accident that we have come across in our lives. That too after spending the better part of our lives together. Only one incident, which has occurred only once, and will never occur again . . ."

Shayela's wild shriek interrupted Mamun. "There are many things in our life which happen only once, they can't happen twice. Our birth, our death. How many times can you die, tell me? But then how can a slimy bastard like you die? You're barely alive!"

Mamun had a tough time accepting his comely, domesticated, pretty-as-a-doll wife was actually uttering these words. He had known Shayela for twenty-two years, but the woman sitting in front of him seemed someone else. Never before had he heard such uncivil words from her. She had been so invisible, so unobtrusive, so restrained in her manners that not once did Mamun have to worry about her while leading his own greedy and lustful life. When Shayela walked, her footsteps never made a sound. When she sat next to the window and brushed her hair, it seemed as though her whole body were made of some magical golden light, just like a piece of sunlight hovering over a white wall. When it was learnt that she was to give birth to a baby, Mamun had felt it was like a virgin becoming pregnant—because he himself could never summon the memory of Shayela's nude body.

The same Shayela was now speaking in the foulest, the most uncouth of tongues. Mamun's hands began to itch—he felt like bringing the whip down from the wall and lashing that wax-like face of hers. He had absolutely no need for a beautiful woman. Nor did he have any need for a chaste one. Chastity was an illusion, no woman carried a brand on her head saying whether she was chaste or otherwise. The home of a statesman was not the appropriate place for a discourse on chastity. Mamun simply didn't have the time or inclination to be drawn into such a conversation.

He remembered that, on the day of the incident, he had been summoned at around nine in the morning, by none other than Him. He was a short man, with trimmed hair, wearing rough and thick everyday clothes, and had a pair of tiny yet eagle-sharp pale yellow eyes. He never uttered a word without smiling first, and yet every time Mamun stood in front of Him, a cold shiver ran down his spine instantly—every single time, without exception. But these days, he felt comfortable speaking to Him. In fact, He had given Mamun the liberty to speak his mind freely, so much so that Mamun often became insolent while presenting his points. But still the cold shiver never left him. When a man smiled, was it really possible for him to completely detach his thoughts and actions from that smile, however fake it may be? It was possible for Him.

That morning, He said, "I hope all the arrangements have been made for the evening. Good. But still, I called you because I want to hear your independent thoughts on the subject. Don't worry about what you would have said in front of others, speak your mind, speak freely, let me know what you think."

"Sir, what can I say now? The decision has already been made. All arrangements for the evening have been completed—I've personally supervised everything. A marquee to accommodate five thousand people, elaborate preparations. Stage, lights, microphone. We've spared no expense. The entire nation knows that tonight you're going to announce the formation of a new political party. What exactly do you want me to tell you now sir?"

For a moment or two, His smile wavered. Black specks of a wormlike darkness seemed to descend upon His face. Sighing, he said, "That's right, I've already taken the decision. It's true, there's no use talking about it anymore. But you tell me, has the decision been a wrong one? If I don't go to the common man, if I don't embrace the common man, how long do you think I'll be able to survive on this chair, how long do you think I can be in power?"

Mamun was busy examining the carpet in His office—he was convinced that the carpet in his own drawing room was just as expensive as this one, if not more. He rubbed his feet on the carpet softly and said, "Sir, since you asked for my honest opinion, I'm obliged to give it to you, but please forgive me for doing so. When the power you speak of hasn't come from the common man, why do you need to embrace him?"

The two pale yellow eyes began to shine brightly. "The common man is the one true source of power. All the power that I have comes from him—that's what I believe."

"Sir, that's what your speech for tonight says. I'm sure you must have read it by now. You yourself asked me to draft it. But sir, your power hasn't come from the common man. And the common man knows that too, in fact he knows it very well. I don't think there's any confusion in the common man's mind about where absolute power lies right now."

"But isn't the military part of the public as well?"

"Sir, of course the military is part of the public, an integral part," Mamun stressed once again. "I'm saying this again sir, I'm going to express my honest opinion only on your command. Even my most independent opinion depends on whether you give me the go-ahead or not."

He said, "I'm exhausted, you know? All this . . . I'm exhausted. And yet I want to listen to what you have to say. But I am not prepared to listen to any nonsense now. We were talking about the military—are you trying to say the men from the military are not citizens of this country? Don't they have their blood relations among the people? Where do you think the military comes from?"

"Sir, there's no need at all for such complicated questions. The crux of the matter is that the people of the country will accept the reign of whoever holds the mantle of power. At least that's what my current understanding of the common man says. The military is an organised force—the public is not. The two do not mix, they will never mix. In fact, I'd go to the extent of saying that although firearms feel cold to the touch, whenever anyone wraps his fingers around the butt of a gun . . . "

"I understand what you're trying to say." The soft smile on His lips had been faint all this time, but now it seemed to broaden. Mamun didn't stop. He stared at His life-size portrait on the wall and said without batting an eyelid, "The common man knows that he is powerless, and he feels it most when the mantle of power is changing hands."

A dark cloud seemed to hover over His face. He said, "I've already told you that I understand what you're trying to say, haven't I? But tell me, how long can one cling on to the power? I know all these fat, greedy, power-hungry bastards—every one of them. Their brains are all mush by now, their souls rotten. And don't think I don't know you—you're also a crook of the first order. It's just that your brain is still functioning, it's still fresh. I can't hope to have a claim on power forever, can I? You know that better than me. The whole world is riding on the waves of democratic principles and republican ideals. You know very well that without external help it's impossible to run the country even for a day, impossible!"

Mamun knew that He was "thinking aloud" right now, and that it was best for him to remain silent at such times. Suddenly He narrowed His eyes and looked at Mamun.

"There's no alternative, absolutely no alternative, to the common man. I have to go to him, I have to embrace him. I've already spoken to all the political leaders of the country—I'm sure you are aware of that?"

Mamun said in an innocent tone, "Yes sir, I do. They have all backed you. In their words, they are happy to extend their support to both your leadership as well as your strategy."

"And I'm trying my best to open a line of communication with the youth of this country."

"Well, the youth are saying that they are right behind you. That's the pulse of the nation sir, you are not alone anymore—whether you want it or not."

He stared at Mamun for some time. Then He said, "I like you. Yes, I like you. But I want you to know this—I haven't forgotten where I come from, I haven't forgotten the common man. The entire nation will back me on this. You'll see that for yourself, tonight, when the leaders of as many as seventy-three political parties merge their parties with my new party."

"Sir, if you permit me to say so—more than half of the seventy-three parties that you referred to just now do not have a single member besides the leader. As for the others, the leaders of some of these parties are joining your party from behind bars, they're in prison. Then there are some who . . . "

"I believe I've already made myself clear that I don't want to hear any nonsense today."

"Certainly, sir, but let's not forget that some of these people you're referring to are now in prison thanks to you. You branded them incorrigibly corrupt and immoral and threw them behind bars as soon as you came to power."

"A man can change, he can have a change of heart . . . "

"That's not my point sir. All I'm trying to say is that I'm a little uncomfortable about the fact that you expect these very people to represent the common man of this country."

"Even a toothless, clawless tiger is a tiger, don't you agree?"

"I fully agree sir, it is such tigers that turn into man-eaters."

"Ah-ha! What do you think I'm going to use them for? Nothing! They'll just pace up and down in their cages all day. Me? I would rather depend on the power of youth. Who do you think is going to take over the reins of the country ten years down the line?"

"The power of youth, the power of old men—whatever you may call it sir—power cannot be divided, power is unity, it is indivisible. That's what British philosopher Hobbes has said."

"Yes, yes, I had read that during my IA—Hobbeys."

"Hobbes."

"Yes, right. Hobbeys."

"Hobbes."

The more Mamun thought about this conversation later, the more astonished he was at his excellent camaraderie with Him. This was unthinkable, really—the trust and faith He had placed in him, the patience with which He had listened to his point of view. Could anyone think of one, just one other, bureaucrat in this country who could boast of the rare fortune of such amity, such cordiality from a man of His stature? Later that evening, Mamun watched Him as He was walking towards the stage. In normal circumstances, he never had the temerity to look at Him directly, but that evening, Mamun took his time to watch Him closely. A short man, dressed in simple clothes, walking swiftly towards Mamun—there was nothing extraordinary about Him. His complexion was quite dark, one shoulder higher than the other, a slight limp, a stumbling gait. He jerked his shoulder every now and then to adjust His collar. There seemed to be a halo round His head and an air of grace and modesty. He walked directly towards Mamun Rasheed with a smile on His face. Was this the same man, the most important man in the country, the epitome of power in this nation, with whom Mamun had spent an hour this morning bantering, laughing and debating? Mamun found it exceedingly difficult to believe it was. A few leaders with sly expressions followed at His heels, struggling to keep pace. He was certainly surrounded by young men, on all sides! Mamun didn't know any of them—they had chains around their necks, bands on their wrists, and were shouting slogans at the top of their voices. "We'll follow you wherever you go." The poor body-guards and police staff were having a tough time, and had been completely sidelined. The youth—yes, the youth had taken up the responsibility of His safety, His well being.

He was all smiles as He walked towards Mamun Rasheed, but it seemed He didn't recognise him, walking right past and on to the stage. And then for five minutes, an earth-shattering voice blared out from the loudspeakers, introducing Him, "Padma, Meghna, Jamuna—like the waters flow free. You lead us to our destiny, for we shall follow thee!"

He rose to His feet and raised his arm to silence the crowd. The marquee had been built to accommodate five thousand peo-ple, and yet it was short of space. People were pushing and jostling and falling over one another. The turnout was unprece-dented. But the moment he raised his arm a strange hush swooped on the crowd and everyone fell silent. Shayela was sitting next to Mamun, her fair swanlike throat lifted, her soft, pure eyes on the stage. Mamun remembered how he had suddenly been stunned by his wife's celestial beauty! And even if it was only for a moment or two, he had bowed to her grace. Then He started His speech, shattering the silence of the evening, shaking the seven-storied building behind the stage to its very foundations. The speech continued.

"And that is why I have come to all of you, to spread a smile of cheer, to offer my undying love, to accept your love with all humility. Come tomorrow morning, we will have to spread out, we will have to roll up our sleeves and step into the innumerable fields and farms of this bountiful nation. Yes, we have to work, work for the betterment of the poor, for the betterment of the downtrodden, for the betterment of us all. There's not a single moment to lose, not a single excuse to offer. Come tomorrow morning, our politics will be the politics of production, our politics will be the politics of output, our politics will be the politics of export, our politics will be the politics of the people . . . "

It had become dark by the time he left. A mildly cold breeze blew through the bushes on the side of the park.

All the lights were turned on in unison. Mamun Rasheed was happy to see the arrangements. They had followed his instructions down to the last word. Bright beams swept the marquee. What an excellent turnout it had been! How beautiful the place looked! If only he could do something about these speeches! Soon after He had announced the formation of a new political party, the cacophony of speeches had started. Mamun could single-handedly choke every one of those scoundrels to death—every one of those who were screeching out those incessant speeches. What if man hadn't had the power to give speeches? Such thoughts were going through Mamun's mind when, all of a sudden, exactly half an hour after He had left—yes, he knew because he had glanced at his watch—all the lights went off at the same time.

What just happened? How did it happen? Mamun turned around and looked into a dark black wall. All those people, the entire marquee—everything had been swallowed by the darkness. And just then he heard the loud noise of an explosion. It was so sudden and so loud that Mamun felt his heart lurching wildly.

He choked. At once a piercing slogan hit his ears—"Padma, Meghna, Jamuna—like the waters flow free. Padma, Meghna, Jamuna—like the waters flow free."

A few men ran towards the stage, a few others climbed on to it from the back. Mamun's eyes had adjusted to some extent to the dark by then. He saw the faint outlines of thousands of men running helter skelter. They screamed and laughed, and then a blinding beam from a flashlight fell on Shayela's face.

"Look, there. A milky one."

Within a fraction of a second, Mamun saw a large hand clutch Shayela's blouse and drag her from her seat. It wouldn't be a lie to say that he had jumped forward to help her, but the flashlight had been switched off by then. He could barely distinguish one person from another in the crowd—he couldn't even make out whether the shadows were real or imaginary, and whether they had weapons in their hands. One of the shadows came up to him and said, "Go home, you son of a bitch. Come back after an hour and take her away."

No sooner had he heard those words than Mamun felt something metallic crash on his right shoulder. Very slowly, someone dropped a soft black curtain on whatever little he could see. His head felt light and he couldn't see Shayela anymore.

Five steely fingers sank into Shayela's skin, almost crushing her bones. Every time she tried to reach out into the darkness for some support, she could touch nothing but the same steely hand that had sunk into her skin. Once or twice, she tried to say, "Who are you? Where are you taking me?" But two strong hands grabbed her and almost squeezed the air out of her chest. Her feet were no longer on the ground. A cruel paw kneaded one of her breasts and a foul smelling face with a pointed beard hovered inches away from hers. All she could see in the dark were a row of white teeth, and someone's hot breath scalding her face—"Shut up, shut up, you whore! Shut up! Or else I'll grab that throat of yours and squeeze the life out of you!"

Shayela's body soon turned numb. Like a fox that vanishes behind a bush with a chicken in its mouth, the man disappeared with Shayela behind the wall of the seven-storied building beside the park. It was then that Shayela realised what was going to happen. She screamed, "Do you know who my husband is? The police will shoot you like a dog."

"No they won't. The man who is guarding us all is the police's daddy, understand bitch? We are the youth of this country. Our party has been formed today—let me have some fun now—mmm . . . "

Jagged tin canisters below her back, shards of glass, chunks of cement and bricks—the dark sky up there, and in that sky, the bright constellation, Orion! For a brief period of time, a wave of light had swept over the area, all the lights had come on for just a few seconds. And in that deluge of light, standing ten feet away, the man who had become visible for just a few seconds—who was he? Was he Mamun Rasheed? All Shayela wanted to know was the answer to that one question—her life and her death depended on the answer. Would anyone tell Shayela who that man was? Anyone? Anyone at all? Shayela would give her whole life to the person who could tell her the truth. Who was that man?

With a frown on her face, and the veins in her temple throbbing visibly along with her heavy breaths, Shayela watched

Mamun as she sat on the bed in what she had called "home" all these years.

Fifteen seconds—yes, that was it, Mamun had calculated later. The lights had come back on for fifteen seconds. What had he really seen during those fifteen seconds? Had he seen a dog kneeling down and feasting on a chunk of flesh? Or had he seen an exposed navel? No, he simply couldn't tell. There were some truths in life which no one dared to face. And anyway, everything had turned dark after fifteen seconds.

THE
DAUGHTER
AND
THE
OLEANDER

The ruthless winter had arrived, cold layers of frosty air were descending upon the earth, the moon shone over the coconut tree. A plantain leaf was tossing and turning in the soft breeze, taking turns to show its back and its front to the onlooker. On the other side of the village, at the bend of the road that led to the town market, dewdrops glistened on the tin roof of Rahat Khan's house. A fox put its front paws up on the steps of Kanu's mother's hut and let out a howl into the night. Its call was immediately answered by a strange sound from within the ruins of abandoned houses that lined the path to the schoolhouse. Resounding cries of "Catch it, catch it, there it goes" echoed through the air. The darkness trembled as the moonshine moistened the tin roof. The killer fox loped up to the road with a chicken in its jaws. The dying creature flapped its wings and cast a shadow on the ground. The fox cast its own shadow too, although it looked like that of a wolf. It looked up at the moon, crossed the road with wolf-like caution and finally disappeared within the bushes. Half a dozen men from Chandmoni's family, sticks and sickles in their hands, stepped up to the road, looking around and swearing under their breath, "Which way did it go, that damned fox? Which way?"

More frost drifted down on the village.

Inam looked down from the big bridge, trying to catch his reflection in the water below. He was the eldest son of Sardar's second wife. He looked for his own face on the silvery surface of the water. The breeze continued to play gently, the dead bark of a chestnut tree tumbled around, the frost continued to wet the ground. A glint of light bounced off the leaves of a wild orange-berry plant. The easternmost branches of the old jackfruit tree waved their arms, just like an ugly old hag beckoning a scared child with her shrivelled hand. The sound of a hundred tambourines filled the air.

Inam moved away from the bridge, climbed down the dusty slopes and stopped by the dry swamp. The white serpentine path in the distance now seemed to wake up from hibernation, as Feku's tiger-like form showed up beyond the bend of the road, with Suhash following him. Busy chatting with each other, they offered no explanation of why they were here in the middle of the night. The conversation had now warmed up around the heavenly puris that Suhash had eaten at his uncle's wedding party. The transistor radio under Feku's arm was switched on, but no one was really listening to it. By the swamp, in the deathly cold, Kanika was making a futile effort to lament the pangs of loneliness. Surprisingly, not a single bird was calling.

"Switch it off," Inam said in irritation.

"There you are!" They stopped. Suhash smiled, exposing his black teeth, stained by the smoke of beedis.

Inam's annoyance had risen further. Once again, he said, "Switch off the radio."

"No one will hear," Feku said, "and even if they do, they won't come this way."

"No, it's not that. I don't like this song," Inam said. Feku turned the knob to squeeze the air out of Kanika's throat.

"All right, now let's go," Feku said as he passed the radio to Suhash. "It's getting late, we should get there before they go to bed."

Suhash took the radio and asked, "Who?"

"The old man, who else?" said Feku, as he spit on the ground. "He goes to bed early."

As they walked on, the wind picked up speed—it was blowing towards them over the swamp. The sound of dry leaves filled the space around them. A large fish splashed its tail on the surface of the water in the Kazis' pond. The Khans were seen gathered around a pot in their yard—they were cooking rice over a coal fire—and as the fire burnt, it illuminated the beautiful faces of the family's daughters.

"Aren't you going to school these days?" Suhash asked.

"No," Inam replied.

"You don't mean to stop studying, do you? Don't do that. You won't get a job."

"Yeah, as if you'll get a job if you study!" Inam said.

Suhash didn't say anything more. He tapped a beat on the radio, casually kicking up dust with his ill-fitting boots. Inam sensed a dry smell as the dust hit his nose. He remembered the scenes that afternoon—the market, the fish. The memory of the fish made him think of the river. It was almost dry now, the sand lay exposed, and people were bringing home cartloads of it. An entire area near the bend of the river was now covered with white catkins. The schoolhouse was visible on the opposite bank, with a bird wagging its long tail on the branch of a large horseradish tree nearby. The brass gong of the school had split into two. A rod had been hung from the ceiling in the veranda. When beaten with an iron rod, it produced a shrill clang, at the sound of which the headmaster—who was an out and out clown—would rush through the veranda, surveying the classrooms. Tarapada "sir" would enter his classroom with a couple of books under his arm, his wrapper thrown around his shoulders, a fountain of words spilling forth through a row of half-broken teeth.

Inam remembered the images that tumbled towards him—just like the dry yellow leaves of the neem tree tumbling in the breeze and falling on the ground below. The images went away just as quickly—like a train speeding over a bridge and through the fields, ignoring the naked boy watching it in wonder. As the visions disappeared, Inam realised that Suhash was still prattling on about his uncle's wedding party. Feku had not heard a word—he was now hanging back to light a cigarette. The glow at the end of the matchstick looked pale in the moonlight, illuminating Feku's ugly face—the scar on his forehead, his lidless eyes like a chicken's, his drooping lips.

"Don't you want one?" Feku asked.

Suhash paused briefly, placed a cigarette between his lips, lit it with another matchstick and resumed his story.

"You need to take a launch to get there, through the Madhumati. We were sailing through the dark night, the banks were lined with heaven knows which villages—someone said it was the Sunderbans. It was so dark, and the jungle was very dense, you know."

Suhash seemed to have been telling the same story since yesterday and could very well continue into the next day too, mused Inam.

"That damned son of a barber," Inam muttered under his breath in frustration. "Just look at him going on and on."

The exaggeration in Suhash's stories was the stuff of legend. This one was no different. It had started with the objective of describing the puris, but had branched out in a hundred different directions, including but not limited to his uncle's joyous expressions at getting married, the history of the alliance, the search for the perfect bride, the tiff between the bride's uncle and the groom's father, the trouble Suhash and his cousins had to face a few hours before the wedding when they went to the local laundry to rent a silk kurta for the groom—all of it was described in vivid detail.

Inam couldn't take it anymore. Turning towards Suhash, he said, "Why on earth did your uncle have to get married?"

"The soft rays of the rising sun glistened on the waters of the Madhumati. My grandfather jumped off the launch when it reached the village. He slipped on the mud and fell flat on his face. And the bride's sisters . . . oh! Don't ask me to tell you how beautiful they are . . . oh!"

Feku had been silent for a long time. Now he blew smoke into the darkness and said, "Where does this uncle of yours live? Make sure you let me know when his sisters-in-law come visiting."

"No sir, you can forget about that," Suhash shut his eyes languorously and shook his head with the air of guarding a vital secret.

"I see. Now I realise why you take a trip to your new aunt's village every week," Feku winked at Suhash. "You don't need to spend a paisa over there, do you? You must be living like a king over there."

Rahat Khan's tin roof was out of sight by now, as were the bridge and the swamp. Chandmoni's men had given up and gone home—after all, how long could one grieve the death of a chicken? Perhaps its shiny feather, or a yellow leg, or a part of its beak would be found the next day—somewhere within the brick kilns of the Basus or the dilapidated ruins of the Sarkars' ancestral home. The men had forgotten the bird, eaten a sumptuous dinner and gone to bed. Only the grand old lady of the house was sitting upright in her not-so-grand shed, pouring oil from the lamp into the cracks of her soles. How the wick was still burning was a matter of cosmic mystery.

"Ooohhh, how cold it is." The old lady shivered and pleaded with her daughter-in-law, "Bou, o bou, give me one more blanket . . . I'm going to die here tonight . . . o bou?"

The daughter-in-law was sunk in the deepest of slumbers, and her husband, though wide awake, muttered to himself, wondering why the hag was still alive. The old woman yelled out one last time, her trembling voice almost inaudible in a sudden gust of freezing wind. Life went on. Feku pursed his lips. Suhash fiddled with the knob of the transistor radio. Inam bowed his head, lost in his thoughts.

They got off the road soon afterwards, walking onto the grass and stamping on the ground to shake off the dust from their shoes. As soon as they entered the bylane on the left they were enveloped by a black shroud of darkness, which blinded them momentarily, while some godforsaken tendrils lashed at their face, startling them. Feku cursed at the vines. Then he calmed down and said, "I wonder why I get caught so often these days."

Suhash's eyes lit up in the dark. "Can I ask you something? Promise not to get angry." Without waiting for Feku's approval, he continued, "How can you stand all the kicks and punches every day? Don't they hurt? My damned brother slapped me the other day, and I swear I couldn't get up for an hour. And you? What the hell are you made of, really?"

Feku nodded, saying, "You need to learn how to absorb the blows, my dear friend. You need to learn it from the experts, just like you go to school for a good education."

Inam flared up once again. "Yes, the teachers are educating the students very well!" He flung an unprintable expletive at the teachers.

Feku continued, "If you're stupid, or if you've never learnt how to absorb pain, then you should never try to pick anyone's pocket on the road—even if you see money sticking out, no, never."

The mention of money made Inam very sad. Edged on by Tendu the driver, he had once dipped his hand into the pocket of a grim-faced gentleman in a crowd. Inam still remembered the deafening rustling of currency notes almost bursting his eardrums that day. The monstrous victim emitted an earth-shattering scream and began to growl in fury. It was only after a few moments that Inam realised that he was actually hacking up phlegm and clearing his throat. So Inam made no money that day. He could always steal coconuts and sell them in the market, but having no rice at home was very painful.

The path was sunk in darkness. A intricate network of vines ran over their heads. Lost in his story, Feku stepped on Suhash's toes, and Suhash yelled out, "Aaooo! Damn . . . my toes . . . "

"Look out, don't drop the radio," Feku said. "You know what happened the other day? I was in a crowded bus, it was running at fifty, maybe sixty. This man in front of me had some money sticking out of the pocket of his kurta. As soon as I touched it he grabbed my hand. And then started beating me up . . . ohhh! It was like a fox entering his pen. See this wound on my forehead? It hasn't healed yet."

"Now this one has started with his stories," Inam thought.

Suhash switched on the transistor radio, and it screeched eerily in the darkness. Suhash spat in the dark and said, "That blasted woman is still singing." He switched the transistor off and let loose his own voice.

"Now that you've come into my life . . . "

A dog ran up to them, trying to yelp along. Unable to harmonise, it rubbed itself against Inam's legs and began shaking its bottom.

"The bitch is trying to warm herself up," Feku remarked, going on to describe how his life was doomed, who the people responsible for the said doom were, how he had learnt the art of picking pockets, how he had sharpened his skills, how he had had a successful run and how, of late, he had been getting thrashed—all of it in vivid detail.

"What else can I do, tell me?" he said. "If only I'd had an education . . . "

"To hell with education, I piss on the face of education," Inam said, irked, as usual.

"In that case," Feku chipped in, "Let's take the high ground and piss on the face of every honest means of earning a living. I mean, think about it. There's nothing we can do—there's just no work. There's no land that we can till. There's no money that we can use to start a business. What the hell can we do?"

Not a single bird could be heard. Whatever sound they could hear was all muffled. They were surrounded by fog and frost. A cat crossed the path ahead, its eyes shining in the dark. Suhash, Feku and Inam had stopped talking. Suhash put the transistor radio under his arm. Feku wrapped the muffler around the lower half of his face. Inam rubbed his palms together to warm them. The Pals lived in the house on the right—they were potters. The house itself was in pretty bad condition. It had once belonged to the Sens, who had left in 1950.

As he walked past the shaddock tree, Inam tore off a leaf and scanned the cold front-yard of the house. The smell of burnt clay hit his nostrils and he could see the black vats lying around. Snoring emerged from beyond the broken door.

"Everyone's fallen asleep," Suhash whispered.

"Hmmm," Feku concurred.

"I told you let's drop it tonight," Feku complained. "I . . . I'm scared."

Feku made a face at Suhash. "Oh you're scared, are you? Poor baby! Go home and suck on your mother's titties."

Suhash said, "Whatever you say, the old man scares me. At times it seems he's going to die any moment. And then it seems he's going to kill us all. Have you seen his face when we enter?"

"Yeah, yeah, shut up now," Feku said dismissively. "Have you seen his face when he gets the money?"

Inam clenched his teeth and felt like choking Feku to death.

But Suhash had switched sides by then. He said with a grin, "You know what the girl reminds me of? Have you seen those tender coconuts? Soft and juicy inside, white flesh waiting to be peeled off? Isn't that right? Huh, tell me?"

Inam felt like killing both of them.

As they walked on, Feku and Suhash began laughing among themselves, falling on each other, cracking up at each other's jokes. Two steps away, the village doctor was sitting inside his house—his large, corpulent, fair frame visible through the open door in the light from the lantern. A single dry leaf was twirling in the breeze on the paved quay by the pond. Then came the open space to the left. The milky white moonlight, made wet by the fog, fell on the stunted dead grass. The rose-apple tree was dark, the background darker, and a deathly silence hung over the expanse. They walked on, crossing, successively, a barren tract of land, a slice of jungle, a cultivation of betel leaves, a forest of catkins, tall grass, a dead pond, and a swamp.

They were now standing next to a bamboo gate. Beyond it lay open land—no flowers or plants had grown there. Inam had lagged behind, so far behind that he could easily turn back. A light with a reddish tinge could be seen behind the wooden bars on the window. The glittering eyes of a fox disappeared within the depths of the dry pond. With an unearthly screech, a hawk announced its presence, cracking a dead branch with its claws before shutting its eyes. Feku held up the bamboo gate and waved at Suhash, who was clutching the transistor radio with one hand and while covering his mouth with the other, refusing to pass. Inam took advantage of the situation and turned to Feku. "Give me a couple of takas, I'll pay you back tomorrow."

Feku let go of the gate and said, "Oh, so you've come to the party empty-handed, huh?"

At that very instant, a golden-hued hand rose in the half-shadow and descended gently on the head, the fingers gently caressing the oily hair, then wiping the oil on the free end of the sari—a sari which Inam himself had got, but had no way of taking off right now. In desperation, he said, "Just two takas, please, I promise I'll pay back tomorrow."

Clenching his radish-like teeth, Feku said, "What, do you think my pockets are bursting? I have only two takas with me right now."

"Then Suhash—you lend me two takas, please. Give it to me please. Please. Who's that goddess of yours, Kali, yes, I swear by Kali, I'll pay you back tomorrow, I promise."

Looking at Feku, Suhash said, "Can you believe this? He never told us a thing! He has been coming along like a goody-goody boy all this while, and now he tells us that his pockets are empty? Stupid, come and put your hands in my pocket. No, no, come, see for yourself. I only have two takas with me—I flicked them from my brother's pocket this morning."

As Inam gave up hope, an old man's voice was heard from beyond the gate, "Who's there? Who are you?"

The reddish light suddenly disappeared from the window and the door opened with a bang. The old man stepped out holding a lantern, casting a long shadow on the yard. He walked through the yard and stood by the oleander next to the gate. Two wizened legs stuck out from under the short lungi. He raised the lantern to the level of his face—a face criss-crossed with innumerable lines resembling the cracks on dry ground at the peak of summer. With cold piercing eyes, he took a long look at Inam, Suhash and Feku. Then he lowered his trembling hand holding the lantern and said, "Oh, it's the three of you. Come in. I wondered who it was. But then, who else could it be? Who'd want to come here in the middle of the night? And for what? No, I was wide awake. I can hardly sleep these days. At my age, one can't sleep at will . . . "

The man continued to blabber mindlessly. "Come inside, it's too cold out there. But then, it's no better inside either, you know? It's all the same, I tell you, all the same. For a man who's had to leave his country, there's no inside and no outside. Everything's the same."

As the three of them walked through the gate, the man tugged at a branch of the oleander. The ground beneath was cold and hard—Inam's heels hurt.

Inside, a black bench was lying in one corner. The chickens cried out in their sleep. A cool breeze blew over the swamp with a shrill whistling sound. The old man settled down on a broken chair and put the lantern on the ground beside him. The three of them pulled the bench closer and sat down. No one talked. The man was clearly asthmatic, his breath shallow and troubled. He had appeared alert earlier, but now he was quiet, breathing with great effort. His unshaven cheeks bore evidence of neglect.

His veins seemed to stick out of the fingers he had now placed on the armrest of the chair. It must have been ages since he had clipped those long dirty nails. Every time some phlegm gathered near his throat, it blocked the passage of air altogether, and the man almost choked. Inam felt an urge to clear his windpipe with a rod or something similar.

"So? What's going on? All well?" The man started speaking in a nearly choked voice. "I think it's about time for me to go now, eh? What do you say? Let's say I die now, at this instant, just like that. Finish! And then? Why do I care? Dang da-dang dang! Leaving that old hag to rot in this hell. Her and her litter. It's only you who come by now and then, you come asking if everything is all right. No time is a bad time for you, my boys. You're always welcome, in fact, what would we do without you? We all adore you, every one of us in the family."

Feku seemed quite frightened by now. He stared into the old man's eyes and tried to assess the situation, and the more he did so, the deeper he shrank back on the bench. Suhash looked at the man with wide eyes, thinking, "He's surely going to kill us tonight. Why did we have to come? We shouldn't have."

"We would have starved to death in this jungle had it not been for you," the old man continued. "We . . . we don't know how to get food from the land . . . we've never known. You have all those wonderful skills, we don't. We're from another country— a dry land. Everything is different there, all our habits are differ- ent. We would have starved to death here, my boys, had you not helped us. The children really love you. Ruku, for instance, my eldest daughter. She's going to make tea for you now."

A big lump of phlegm clogged his windpipe, and the old man rolled his eyes and almost coughed his lungs out. What was it? He had been chattering a moment ago and now—was he going to die? Suhash and Feku waved their arms, yelling, "No, no, we don't want tea, thank you."

"You don't?" The man seemed to have controlled himself. "Very well."

The wind began to blow again over the top of the peepal tree, swirling down, advancing towards them, bringing with it the distant sound of tambourines and the musical lore of Vishakha and Tamal—and then, just like that, the sound was gone. A new sound was heard now—the rubbing of two currency notes, under Suhash's shawl. Feku took the two notes from Suhash, added his own money to it and crumpled it all into a ball. He hesitated, bit his fingers, and then seemed to make up his mind. He bent towards the old man and said, "This is from Suhash and me."

The man was close to falling off his chair with a start, rattling its legs. "From you? From Suhash and you? All right. I wonder how much more I'll keep borrowing from you. I don't know when I'll be able to repay your debt."

Suhash rose from the bench. The old man quickly said, "Are you leaving? Don't go—Ruku will be upset. You didn't even let her make some tea for you. If you leave without meeting her, she will never speak to me again. Wait."

The old man entered the hut, his shadow merging into the darkness within. The chickens cried out once again, and an old woman's voice was heard, her sharp tongue lashing out in the darkness, "Shut up, shut up, you whore. Shut up, or they'll hear you, bitch." The deathly silence returned to the yard.

The old man stepped out of the hut, his head bowed, his shoulders drooping. He walked up to the bench and whispered, "Go inside, she's waiting for the two of you. Yes, in there. Inam, you sit down. Let's talk."

The old man began to talk. The cold was gnawing away at his skin, and the shawl was just not helping. He could cope with the cold, but his phlegm would just not let him speak.

"When I first came here, you know, when I first came here," the man gasped for breath, trembling violently. "The first time I came here . . . " He struggled to finish. "First time, when I came . . . here . . . to live in this hut . . . I planted an oleander . . . ."

The sound of someone weeping emerged from the darkness inside the hut, accompanied by the tinkling of bangles and the rustling of a sari. A flawless, golden body began to take shape inside Inam's head. Suhash was laughing in the dark—nasty, obnoxious laughter, like a hyena's.

"I planted an oleander, you know?" The old man paused to catch his breath. He heard the sound of weeping, and then the sound of the laughter. "Not for the flower, but for the seeds, understand? The seed of the oleander. You can get a powerful poison from the seed of the oleander."

As the sound of the whimpering wafted into the yard again, the man's face seemed to be swept away, appearing blurred. "So when I first came here, I planted an oleander, out there, and— you're crying now? You're crying now? Now you're crying?"

THE

IMMIGRANT

He raised his ears and tried to listen. For a sound. Any sound. But there was nothing to listen to. Neither the sound of the wind, nor the sound of dry leaves falling. Nothing at all. The ground was turning ice-cold very quickly. The colourless leaves had been bathed by the silent dew. The chilly wind was blowing in from the north, announcing the not-so-distant end of winter that year. It had found no obstacle on its way. It had whistled past him mercilessly all day long, sucking the last bit of warmth out of his body. And then came fresh blasts of wind—stronger, colder and more cruel than ever before. But just as dusk had begun to fall, the wind, with a few dying flaps of its wings, had sunk into an eerie stillness. As if in mourning, everything around him had fallen silent—the large open fields extending all the way to the horizon, the swamp with the thin layer of water standing on the muck, the unknown, unnamed, colourless, dying shrubs of thorn, everything. Sparing his immediate vicinity for some unknown reason, the fog had settled down everywhere else like the phlegm of a pneumonia patient. Yes, it was the fog that seemed to have replaced the wind. And with it came the deathly silence. He pricked up his ears again for a sound. Any sound in a universe full of sounds. But he couldn't hear anything. Drawing his old and tattered shawl closer around himself, he sank his elbows into the thin layer of yellow grass on the uneven ground, raised his head, and stared at the wall of fog around him.

While it was true that at this moment he could hear nothing but the beating of his own heart, it was also true that throughout the day—and for the better half of the evening, for that matter—there had been no dearth of sounds floating around. He could hear buses and trucks speeding along a distant road somewhere. He had even heard the shrill hoot of a train's whistle. With dusk falling over the secluded field, he had seen a murder of crows flying over his head, cranes flying in pairs, a white breasted kite, a couple of small birds and, finally, a huge unknown bird, barely flapping its wide-spanned wings, gliding parallel to the ground with its feet tucked in, moving its beautiful head left and right. It came from the west and slowly disappeared in the eastern corner of the sky. Meanwhile, hundreds of birds, both big and small, had started chirping and chattering among themselves in the bamboo grove before turning in for the night. But as the night became darker, he didn't hear any more of these sounds. He was shivering in the cold by then, trying to cover the gaping hole in his shawl with his lungi and almost becoming naked in the process. The cold bit into his skin, and pangs of hunger bit into his being. As he pulled out a tiny and dirty bundle of flattened rice, shoved some of it into his mouth and began to chew, he told himself, "They must have fallen asleep by now."

And then, for a long time, he didn't think of anything else. Very carefully, he cupped his palms and gathered a small portion of water from the thin layer over the mud in the canal, and quenched his thirst with it. Then he started walking, or rather, tottering. When the cold became unbearable, when his head felt like a slab of ice, when his feet became numb, he took shelter in a dry ditch like a wounded animal. He lay there in the dark, drawing his knees up to his chest, curling up in a foetal position in search of a little warmth. As the cold wore off, he could think clearly again. "Must be quite late at night now. I wonder how far I've walked. God knows where I am right now. And this cold . . . "

As he lay face down in the dark ditch in the middle of the reaped field, the first thoughts of winter went through his mind. He heard a voice in his head, a man's voice, shouting, "Bashir! Bashir! You're still sleeping? You've had it today. The boss is going to chop your ears off today. You and your damned sleep! Bashir!" He heard the cry just once before everything fell silent again.

The winter could be said to be particularly severe this year. It had arrived early, sometime in early November, but it just wasn't showing any sign of leaving, even with February almost on its way out. It had rushed in even before the early signs of its onset could be felt, sinking its teeth into people's flesh. Like every other year, this year too the aged people began to say, "What a nasty winter it's been this year, really. I've never seen it so cold in all these years of my life."

And like every year, this time too the young men had shut their eyes, shaken their heads and dismissed these claims with smiles. "It's not like that, that's just what you think. Just as we don't feel the cold as much as you do, when you were our age, you wouldn't have felt it either. This is nothing, the real thing is time."

One of the listeners had nodded. "You could be right, you know. The real thing is time. When I was of your age I used to work in the fields in the middle of the night, even at the peak of winter. I used to wake up with the morning star in the eastern sky and set out for the fields at the crack of dawn. Nothing could put me down. You're right, that is the real thing—time. And age."

But two or three old men had disagreed and finally it was their opinion in the matter of the unprecedented harshness of the winter this year that had finally held ground. It was true, everyone said—this year was particularly bad. Especially in the heartlands on the western bank of the great river, where the cold seemed to be pouring down from the skies. The chilly winds from the north had blown relentlessly throughout the day and cast a shadow of gloom over the icy-cold bodies of the villagers, and as soon as the winds had died down in the evenings, the ground had frozen. Who could say that this was the land where the ground had always been white? Because it looked black this year, thanks to the cold. It was impossible to mistake the black as a layer of moss collected over the surface of the ground.

The work had started this year under such frigid conditions. After all, how could the cruelty of nature compete with pangs of hunger? The winter could do its worst, but man had decided to reap whatever little harvest he could, more than half of which had to be deposited in the landowner's granary. Even in its most cruel form, winter was powerless against such resilience.

As a result, not a single sickle in the village could be found lying idle—as usual. Old and tattered shawls, dirty smelly quilts and other such ineffective weapons were employed, and the brave men held their ground as the freezing winds rushed in from the north. The sickles began to turn silvery-white in colour in less than a month. Thankfully, the crops had been harvested and packed by then. Like hundreds of dead soldiers lying on the battleground, the bundles lay on the ground for a couple of days. The work with the sickles having officially ended, the people started piling the bundles in the landowner's granary.

The last trace of green had disappeared from the flat of the plains by then, and the ditches and canals held nothing but dark mud. Snipes poked the slush with their long beaks throughout the day. Black and white cranes stood on one leg in the middle of the muck. The entire land seemed to shrink under the effect of the northern winds. Plants and trees were left standing in the nude. Owing to its camouflaging skills, the green dragonfly transformed itself into an ugly brown insect.

A faint picture of the winter now began to appear on the rough canvas of his ill-bred mind. Accuracy may be the highlight of the above description, but depth of emotion and warmth of feelings were the highlights of the picture. And so, even if he had unintentionally ignored a few details, he did make up for them with the richness of emotion, making the picture an undeniable truth. And no sooner had he imprinted the image in his mind than he made a valiant effort to glance upward from the dark ditch in this godforsaken and ice-cold field. A seemingly impenetrable wall of fog met his eyes. That's all he could see. The plains stood motionless and still. And now, instead of offering him the warmth of a shelter, the ditch began to gnaw away at his flesh with its icicle-like teeth. Even as his eyelids drooped and he was about to faint, he heard a voice shouting in the dark, "Bashir! Bashir! You're still sleeping? You've had it today. The boss is going to chop your ears off today."

The owner of the voice never had to shout very long. Bashir would pull himself away from the warmth of his wife's body in an instant. A soft plump arm would fall on the cold floor with a fleshy sound. His eight-year-old son would slip out of the blanket. Bashir would immediately put him back into its warmth and replace his wife's arm gently across her breast. He would get out of bed carefully, take the shawl hanging from the rope running from one wall of the room to the other, and cover himself with it from head to toe. He would collect his sickle, gleaming in the dark, from the corner, part the door a little and sneak out.

"Is that you, Chacha?"

"Yes my boy, yes. I have been calling you forever! You and your bloody sleep!" Wajaddi would make no attempt to hide the annoyance in his voice. "Come on, let's go. It's already quite late. Bishe Master is not what you may call a good man, you know. Those Santhals he has brought over from the other side—they and those bitches of theirs hardly sleep at night. They drink and cavort and then head out to the fields before the moon sets. What are we to do? We have no option but to show up too, in this biting cold. Now come on, don't just stand there."

"Wait a minute." Bashir seemed relaxed. "Let me have a smoke first."

"We're getting late. You can smoke, I'm going."

"Hang on, Chacha, what's the rush? It won't take even a minute."

"Bishe Master will also take less than a minute to throw us out."

"As if I care! Is there any dearth of work in winter? Everyone needs us. To hell with your Bishe Master."

Bashir tore off a thin stalk of straw from the bundle in the corner and placed it on his palm. Then he started rolling it into a small ball, taking his time to rub it on his left palm with his right thumb. "I'm not stepping out of the house without a smoke."

The repeated mention of a smoke in this cold that cut to the bone was enough to break old Wajaddi's resolve too. He sat down in one corner of the veranda and said, "All right, all right, I'll take a couple of drags if you insist. That's enough now, put it in."

Bashir had pulverised the ball of straw by now. He placed it in the chillum and slapped it hard so that the dust settled down. Then he picked up a piece of flint and a stick of spongewood from the window sill and lit the chillum with his deft hands. Wajaddi looked on patiently even as a chilly gust of wind swept over the hut and shook him to his old bones. The sound of men waking up in the neighbourhood began to waft through the air. Dozens of people emerged from their houses with gleaming sickles and started walking along the path in small groups—some headed towards their own land, some headed to others'.

Bashir kissed the hookah a couple of times, took a single drag to satisfy himself that the contents were all right, and then handed it over to Wajaddi.

Wajaddi puffed away for almost three minutes, and finally said from behind a screen of smoke, "It's not a good idea to leave home without a smoke."

"See? What did I tell you? And there you were, standing in the cold and going on and on about your stupid Bishe Master!"

"When are you going to reap your own crop?" Wajaddi asked.

"It's just a little bit, Chacha—how long will it take, after all? It's the beginning of the season, I think I'll work on others' fields for a few days, you know. I need the money. How about you? When are you reaping yours?"

"Mine? Here, take the hookah. Mine? My crop reminds me of an old man who is about to die of dysentery! Just a few stalks, that too, bent by the wind. I chopped it all off a long time ago and stored it. Haven't you seen the pile? It's massive! You can see it from the next village! Satisfied?"

"I'm sorry, I didn't mean to . . . "

"Come on now, let's go. We're late already."

"All right, let's go."

The two men set off for the day's work. A question flew out of a mound of fog in the distance. "Who's that?" Evidently there was a small cohort of people behind the fog.

"Is that you, Bhakta?" Wajaddi threw a question of his own back at the mound.

"Oh Wajaddi Chacha? Who's that with you?"

"It's me, Bhakta," Bashir replied.

"Oh! Which field?"

"Jamtala. And you?"

"Bherendagarh. Whose field is it?"

"Bishe Master's. What about your own crop, Bhakta? Have you harvested it already?"

"Yes, I have. I'll start piling it the day after tomorrow. Why don't you come over and help me with the threshing?"

"Of course, of course, why not?"

Bashir and Wajaddi walked on. There was still some time to go before morning came. The fog was thinning down. The black ground was wet and rock-hard. Smoke was billowing out of cowsheds all around them and mingling with the fog. There was a heavy screen of fog along the verge that separated the road from the fields. Bashir and Wajaddi walked into the curtain and emerged on the other side. Wet and flattened paddy stalks impeded their progress. A chilly wind began to blow, and the rice plants rustled.

This was all the sound that could be heard in the enormous open field. Only the faint shadowy forms of men could be seen walking through the foggy jungle of grains. And then, as the golden rays of the morning sun tore through the curtain of fog and illuminated the field, the huge field turned out to be teeming with men. A loud, deep and sonorous hum began to reverberate through the skies. It didn't have a name. One could call it the humming of life, of staying alive—warm, feverish, everlasting.

As he lay in the ditch and remembered those days, he felt as if he was dying. He didn't know what happened to a man when he was dying. But he had heard that just before someone died, his entire life flashed before his eyes. He would have no thoughts, nor would he feel any pain or joy. He would only be able to look at all those images from his entire life rushing past his eyes. He, too, could barely think. Like his body, the cold seemed to have frozen his mind too. Nor did he feel any pain or joy, as if he had gone well beyond those feelings. He lay there, not making any effort to shield himself from the cold, gazing helplessly at different images from his life as they brushed past him in the dark field.

Their colours were bright and distinct. They felt real. He could hear, touch, feel everything—the farmland, the men, the trees, the sky.

The hacking of the sickles merged with the hum of the men, the cracking sound of dry snails or tiny crabs being crushed to death under rock-hard feet, the field rats scampering through the blades of paddy, a few enthusiastic farmhands singing at the top of their voices, the sound of the reaping, the bustle of tying up bundles of grain and then the process of piling it all up, the creaks of the grain-laden buffalo carts, the screams of the oil-thirsty wheels, the threshing of the stalks, and a thousand other sounds and images from his village began going through his mind. As the day would progress, the sweet and soft reddish tinge to the sunlight would step aside fearfully to make way for the bright white incandescence that would bear heavily down on the men, slowly reducing both their tempo and their voice—until, soon, only an empty silence hovered over the fields, amidst the glint of the afternoon sun shining off a hundred sickles all at once.

And then, along with these fondly familiar images came another one. Shuddering from head to toe, he tried to push it away, shake it off his mind, smear it with the darkness around him. But it stayed, forceful and clear.

Everyone had returned from the fields that evening. The Santhal men and their women were roasting rats and squirrels, skinning them carefully. The peasants were totting up the day's harvest. It was well past dusk—Bashir and Wajaddi had just finished their work and were hurrying home. Neither of them was speaking. The ground beneath their feet was ice-cold. After some time, Bashir said, "Chacha?"

"Hmmm?" Wajaddi seemed lost in his thoughts.

"O Chacha?"

"What is it?"

"What's all this I'm hearing?"

"Why, what have you heard?"

"Haven't you heard?"

"About what?"

"There's going to be trouble, they say."

"Where?"

"You're saying you haven't heard anything?"

"No, nothing at all."

"What a strange man you are, Chacha! Everyone's been talking about it all day—whispers, murmurs—and you haven't heard anything? They are hacking the Hindus in Pakistan to death. And Musalmans are being slaughtered in Kolkata."

"Who said that? Who?" Wajaddi snarled at Bashir.

"Everyone!"

"Let them say whatever they want to. Go home. Have your dinner and go to bed."

"But they said there'll be an attack tonight. Our village . . . "

"Are you an idiot or something?" Wajaddi snapped at him. "People say all kinds of things, and you believe them? What, what will happen to our village tonight, huh?"

"They'll come."

"Who? Who'll come?"

"The Hindus—from Nawabpur, Srishtidharpur. They'll offer their prayers to Maa Kali and then they'll come."

"Go home." Wajaddi frowned in irritation and reprimanded Bashir.

"People are saying, that's why I thought . . . "

"Oh shut up. It's far too cold . . . "

They walked on in silence for some time. Then Bashir said, "Chacha, I have a feeling it will start all over again."

"What a stubborn ass! Going on and on and on . . . "

Bashir didn't pay any attention to Wajaddi. He said in a whisper, almost to himself, "After all, Pakistan is the land of Musalmans. Musalmans rule the country."

"Then why didn't you go to Pakistan?"

"Do you really think I have the guts to take my family and belongings and set out for such a faraway place? But it's true— that country . . . "

Suddenly, Wajaddi turned around to look at Bashir. Bashir stared blankly at the old man, who seemed to tremble in rage. Finally, Wajaddi said, "How many fathers do you have? How many? How many mothers, tell me? One—right? Just like that, you have only one country—understand? Now go home." Wajaddi walked away abruptly and vanished in the darkness.

But they did come. From faraway villages, leaving the warmth of their homes, with scarlet vermilion smeared on their foreheads, they came in hundreds to kill unknown men, women and children. For almost three hours before they came, Bashir and the other villagers lay in their cold beds and listened to conches being blown and drums being beaten. These sounds travelled through the dark fields, tore through the heavy curtains of fog and whiplashed the trembling village. Like a monstrous eagle, the dark night clutched the settlement in its ugly claws.

It took them minutes to tear through the flimsy defence. The bullock carts blocking the roads were destroyed, and then, in front of Bashir's eyes, Wajaddi was slaughtered. As raging fires danced on the thatch roofs of the huts, Bashir watched the faces of the strangers in horror—their eyes bloodshot, the brand of vermilion on their foreheads, Wajaddi's blood on their faces. Then he looked down on Wajaddi's face—shocked, horrified, dead.

"Bashir! Bashir! They went towards your house!" Someone yelled.

"What? When?"

"My house too . . . everyone . . . everyone's gone . . . "

"Rakib! Rakib! There they are . . . "

Bashir ran. He ran as fast as he could. But by the time he reached his hut, it had been burnt to the ground. His eight-year-old son was in the yard, pinned to the ground by a spear driven through his little chest. The black charred body of a young woman lay still in the middle of the rubble, the air pregnant with the strong smell of burnt flesh.

"Allah! They say you live inside every human heart." Bashir screamed into the blackness of the night. "Where are you tonight? Where are you? Where are you?"

He stood up. It seemed to him that he had been lying in the ditch for aeons, watching his life flash past his eyes. But unable to discard the final, most horrific image, he straightened his frozen limbs and stood up. The veins of his throat began to swell. He raised his hands—they were frozen stiff. He had been lying in the ditch for a long time. Before that, he had been running and walking all through the day, and the day and night before that, and the one before that. He had left his country behind, he had come a long distance from his village. Not once had he tried to make contact with another human being. Not once had he asked for help, or food, or water, or shelter. Not once had he begged or prayed—not even to god. He had said to himself, "I am not Bashir anymore. Bashir is dead. Bashir is done. Bashir doesn't belong to any country. Bashir will now be reborn."

He had spent the better part of the day lying behind a bush and listening to the sounds of the universe. Soft sounds, loud sounds, nearby sounds, distant sounds. He had merged these sounds with his meaningless thoughts. The cold north wind had been blowing all day. The wind had died down in the evening, and a wave of cold had swept over the plains. The ground had frozen, a thick blanket of fog enveloping him. The world around him had fallen silent, and he hadn't even noticed at first. When he finally did, he had pricked his ears up for a sound—any sound. But he had heard nothing. And then he had taken shelter in the ditch. But now, as he hoisted himself out of it, it seemed to him that he was near the border of another country. Unknown even to himself, he would now step on foreign land any minute. He realised he had to be very, very careful.

He didn't want to be seen. He had heard somewhere that men were allowed neither to leave their own country, nor allowed to enter another country. He was afraid that any moment a strong beam of light would fall on his face and blind him, that he would hear a rumbling sound and his lifeless body would collapse on the ground.

An extraordinarily strong gust of cold wind came at him, cutting through his flesh and bones and striking at his marrow. A sensation of pain swirled in every cell of his brain. And then the wind dropped, and his limbs became numb. But he continued to walk. Or so it seemed to him. His legs did move forward, practically detached from his body, and he dragged them along almost like a machine. Suddenly, he stumbled on a stone and fell facedown, and quite against his will, began to roll along the hard ground. After some time, he found his body lodged in a dry canal. He was now convinced that he was dying.

In all probability, he was dying. Nothing around him was alive. The fields, the dry swamp, the canal, the bushes, the skies—everything was dead, there was no hope left in any of them. The east bank of the canal was so high that he couldn't see anything beyond. The world suddenly seemed to have shrunk to a space within the canal, and he prepared to die.

A thin sliver of the moon, ugly and yellow, had risen in the sky. In the moonlight, a pair of feet made its way through the open field and all the way to the crest of the east bank of the canal. A man! Wrapped in an old dirty shawl, with two dark dhoti-clad legs sticking out. A short curved pole was placed firmly on his shoulder, with two baskets hanging from its ends. An axe gleamed in the moonlight in one of the baskets, while the other held a few tools. Bashir looked up in confusion and saw the man. Deep in the canal, he had been seeing the images in his mind once again. The flat plains of his country, the open fields, the humming of the farmhands, his hut—and then he had seen the same hut covered in hungry flames, Wajaddi's eyes like those of a dead fish's, his little boy pierced with a spear, his twenty-six-year-old wife lying like a lump of coal.

Suddenly an earth-shattering scream filled the depths of the canal. Bashir clambered out of the darkness and confronted the dazed man. Two strangers stared at each other's faces in the moonlight. Bashir looked at the man's dhoti, his shawl, the baskets hanging from his shoulder. He

felt a rush of blood to his head, spreading all over his body.

"Bashir! Bashir!"

Someone screamed his name. Bashir saw his son's corpse, his wife's charred remains. In a flash of a second, he hefted the heavy axe in the man's basket, raised it above his head and brought it down with all his might on the man's head. A cracking sound filled the air, much like a thunderclap, and with a shocked, horrified and piercing death-scream, the man dropped dead on the ground, rolling into the canal.

"Bloody pig! You were trying to run away from this country, weren't you? Bastard!" Bashir bared his teeth like a mad gorilla. They shone in the faint moonlight.

Two strong beams of light fell on the open field, one on Bashir, the other on the dead man's face. And in that light, Bashir saw, much to his horror, that the man's face had the same shocked and horrified expression that he had seen on Wajaddi's. The thick veil of fog suddenly seemed to lift, and his tears blurred his vision of both the worlds—the one he was leaving behind, and the one he was headed to.

THE

SORCERER

They say that after every harvest the earth turns into a virgin once more. She has to be wooed, coaxed and cajoled—all over again. One has to express one's loyalty to her, serve her with undying love. And then, with the first showers of the monsoon, she becomes fertile, all the beauty of her youth bursting forth. Wet and dripping, she announces her readiness to accept the seeds of nature, to give life, to hold the fruit of the harvest in her womb.

That year, when the first heavy rains of the monsoon had filled the ponds, rivers, ditches and canals to their brims, when patches of darkness had gathered over the flowing river, when the wailing of the wind had been heard along the forests of the shore, that night, the old sorcerer passed away.

The rains had just set in, and then there was this. The villagers were terrified, they felt restless.

The old sorcerer had been a legend. Like the one-hundred-year-old man from the fairy tales who knew everything. He knew magic spells which could bring down lightning upon earth from the skies, which could make a flying bird turn into stone in mid-air and drop dead on the ground.

He had survived two entire generations. The deaths of his two aged sons had taken place a long time ago, so far in the past that they had almost been erased from the public memory of the village. His three grandsons were still alive—the eldest would turn forty next year.

The villagers were so afraid of the sorcerer that they didn't dare let him live in the village. They had found him a tamarind tree next to a dark dank swamp on the outskirts, and had built a hut for him under it. Actually, it would be wrong to say that they had built a hut for him, for in fact he had built it for himself.

At dusk, far away in the village, the shivering inhabitants could see the frightening man—more than six and a half feet tall, a skeletal silhouette against the grey sky, eyes burning like lumps of coal, a short stick in his hand, pointing upwards and muttering to himself. During the day he could be found lying in one corner of the hut, coiled like a snake. No one dared disturb him unless an exorcism or something of the sort had to be performed.

That night, the sorcerer's grandsons were called for—summoned by some unknown entity. The first heavy rains of the monsoon were underway. Burning with desire, the earth had drunk the streams of water to her heart's content and was now waiting like a benumbed woman. The eldest grandson Raham moved his sleeping wife's hand from his chest and got out of bed. Like a man possessed, he tottered out of the house and disappeared into the darkness. A gust of moist wind blew over the canal towards him, bringing sharp drops of rain that seemed to pierce his skin like a thousand needles. He staggered on through the darkness in the downpour, braving the wind that tried to halt him, through the woods and between the ghostly trees that towered over him, towards the dingy hut by the swamp, until he heard an enraged but muffled hiss below his bare feet. It didn't take even a moment to realise that Raham had stepped on the head of a snake. Like a whip, the slithering snake wrapped itself around his leg, squeezing with all its might. His right leg gradually became numb. But he knew very well that if he lifted the pressure off the serpent's head, death was certain.

The snake unwrapped itself and tried to attack his leg. But Raham's firm, ugly and monstrous feet were crushing the serpent's skull. Gradually, the snake released its grip. Raham gnashed his teeth in the rain and muttered, "Filthy vermin, you think you can kill me?"

With a final spasm running down the length of its body, the snake became still and sank back in the wet grass. Raham lifted his feet, picked the snake up by its tail, and flung it into the swamp.

He continued to walk along in a daze. When he entered the hut, it was to hear a faint trembling voice in the darkness, "It's time for me to go now. Yes . . . it's time, you understand? Have you come? All three of you?"

Raham strained his eyes but couldn't see the sorcerer. It seemed the old man had merged into the darkness. Trying to move forward, he tripped on something and collapsed on the thin bamboo wall to the west. Raham shrieked in horror. But he wasn't injured. He got to his feet, rubbing his eyes. As his vision adjusted to the absence of light, he saw the faint outline of two small mounds of darkness, sitting still on the ground. From the darkest corner of the hut, he heard the old man's voice again. "All three of you are here? Good."

Raham realised that the two heaps of darkness were nothing but his two brothers—Ali and Rameez. It seemed someone had stitched their lips up with needle and thread. Raham grumbled, "Idiots! Can't you speak up? I nearly had a heart attack."

A blinding flash of lightning lit up the entire village—the houses and the lanes, the river and the ominous swamp, and, finally, the sorcerer's wizened and ghastly face. Tearing through the thunderclap, the old man's hoarse voice shook the walls of the dingy shack, "Get out, get out all of you, get away from me . . . "

He waved his shrivelled hand furiously as he spoke. Trembling in fear, the three brothers were about to leave when the old man called after them. "No, not you . . . come back. I'm talking to them. Yes, them. Get out, the lot of you. I've spent my entire life with you. Now that my end is near, let me spend some time with humans. Go now."

Yelling at his invisible companions, commanding them to leave, he finally broke down.

A cold wind blew out of the door towards the swamp with a whistling sound. Raham saw a branch of the tamarind tree break as there was a crack of thunder and a blinding flash of lightning.

The three brothers sat motionless, waiting. The sorcerer whispered, "They're gone now. Listen, I want to tell you something tonight. You know me as your grandfather, but in reality, I'm not related to anyone. I, Rajab Ali, the sorcerer. No one knows when I was born, but I'm going to die tonight. I was the king of ghosts, the master of jinns, everyone bowed before me. But beware, there's someone who has been trying to harm you. He didn't dare come near you while I was alive, but after tonight, he'll try and slaughter you."

Lightning struck somewhere nearby before the old man had finished, and in the white light that filled up the room, Raham thought he saw a strange smile on the sorcerer's lips. None of the three brothers was in a position to speak. The old man continued, "But don't be afraid, I'll teach you a spell. That bastard won't be able to harm you in any way. You'll get anything you want—money, gold, women, anything. But I can't teach the spell to all of you. Only one of you can learn it. Now tell me who wants to learn the spell. Tell me quickly."

For the first time that night, the youngest brother Rameez growled like thunder, "Me . . . I'll learn the spell."

Everyone was silent for a moment or two. Then Ali's voice was heard. "No, I'll learn the spell."

A sharp cruel smile appeared on the dying man's face. He said once again, "Take a decision quickly. I'm going to die any moment. Tell me whom I should pass the spell on to. Anyone who doesn't know this spell is doomed. The one who knows it will rule the world—gold, money, women . . . ."

Rameez's voice rang out like the roar of a lion, "Stay out of this, you two. I'll learn the spell."

"Not in your lifetime. I'm the one who'll learn it."

The old man spoke again, his voice faint and dying, "Hurry!"

The middle brother Ali took a few steps towards the dark corner where the old man was lying. Like a silent predator, Rameez pounced on Ali's neck. Raham sat in his place in silence, watching the two of them fight. Let alone talk, they could hardly breathe. The grabbed each other and rolled around on the floor. The western wall of the hut was the weakest of the four, breaking into pieces when they smashed into it like two monsters. A blind kick from Rameez's strong leg in the dark struck the old man in the belly, and he fell with a muted groan near the eastern wall of the hut.

It seemed to Raham that the fight would never end. He had waited far too long, and was sick and tired of it all by now. So he jumped to his feet, grabbed his two brothers by their necks and pushed their faces into the floor. When they stopped resisting, and Rameez was sure he could safely let them go, he let up on the pressure. Then he left the hut without a word. By then the dawn air had turned ice-cold, with both the rain and the lightning continuing.

At daybreak the villagers found out what had happened.

The sorcerer's feeble hut had indeed collapsed. The old man's body lay in one corner in the mud and grass, his wrinkled skin ashen in the rain. In the other corner, the two brothers Ali and Rameez lay sprawled on the ground, as though badly hungover after a night of wild abandon. A trickle of blood had flowed out of Ali's nose, clotting into a pool overnight, while two of Rameez's teeth were broken. There were fingerprints and bruises on both their throats. Who would have thought something like this could happen at the onset of the monsoon?

At around ten in the morning, Rameez and Ali sat up. The three brothers settled their disagreements mutually, after which Raham told the villagers a hair-rising story.

"As soon as the sorcerer said he would teach us the spell, and that no jinn or ghost would be able to harm us anymore, that we'd never have to worry about money anymore, oh lord, I can't tell you, a small stick, about the size of my finger, came flying through the air and set itself down. And do you know what I saw after that? A little puddle of water had formed around the stick. And then the sorcerer said, there's a jinn who's troubling us. It will surely kill us if we don't learn the spell. And then all

of a sudden, right out of nowhere, a flood came and filled up the room."

"So you didn't get a chance to learn the spell?"

"The spell? Are you crazy? I ran out of the hut to save my life."

Rameez told the rest of the story. "Ten fingers clutched my throat like iron pincers."

Ali said, "Yes, mine too."

Ever since they heard the story, a fear seemed to shadow them wherever they went. They couldn't shake it off no matter how hard they tried. Moreover, the sky looked so ominous that they couldn't tell whether it was day or night. Dark clouds had formed overhead, threatening to burst. They could barely see one another's faces. But the storm had stopped, as had the wind. The tiny leaves stood perfectly motionless and still.

Then came the rain. And what rain! It was impossible to step out. The sorcerer's body had been laid on a bed of hay. The corpse had stiffened by now. Big fat monsoon flies began to buzz around it. A few villagers had gathered outside the hut in the flowing mud. They had to do something about the body. After all, he was widely feared and respected as a guardian of the village, protecting it from evil spirits.

But a strange fear seemed to rob them of speech. They had been sitting there in the mud for a long time. Some of them had put their heads between their knees and started to snooze. Finally Barkat said, "The sorcerer was a Musalman, wasn't he?"

"Why?"

"No, I mean he used to speak to ghosts and spirits and deities. He used to chant mantras all the time—I've even heard he used to visit the cremation grounds."

"Ah, that's how they are, these sorcerers. But then I'm sure his belief in Pir-Munshi and Allah-Rasool was intact. It may not be wise to question his faith."

"Yes, but how can he believe in two faiths? Isn't that considered inauspicious?"

Raham jumped up angrily, saying, "You're making a big mistake if you think you can get away by not giving the man a proper burial. Don't forget he can easily let his jinn loose on all of you."

The vision of the men gathered outside the hut was blocked by the heavy rain, but the backdrop of the serpentine canal, the peculiar tree and the deadly swamp made them feel as though they were sitting in an unreal world. Kobad Sheikh twisted the curly end of his yellow beard and suddenly broke into a chant of Allah, Allah.

The men trembled and nodded. "No, no, we have to give him a burial. How can we not?"

But it soon became obvious that they had left it too late and that the dead sorcerer had already let his trusted jinn loose on the village. As many as three graves were dug, but the sorcerer could not be buried. Every time they dug, water would gush out from the earth below and fill the hole.

The storm raged on in drunken fury. The wind wreaked havoc on the flimsy huts. Lightning struck the top of a coconut tree. In the end they had no other option but to hold the sorcerer's corpse down in a watery grave and pour mud and wet earth over him. Raham commented on the half-baked job, "The old man's grave will go up in flames tonight. No matter how much it rains, the grave will burn."

Fear! Fear! Fear! A terrible, horrendous, formless, shapeless fear. The day passed under the cloud of this fear.

Raham curled up in his bed at night, petrified at the thought that none of the three brothers had learnt the spell. If only the two pigs hadn't fought each other! They hadn't paid attention to the many wonders of the spell, going at each other's throats as soon as women were mentioned. Moreover, Raham knew very well that it was Rameez's kick that had killed the old man, because he had not made a sound after collapsing. Raham glanced at Ali and Rameez every now and then.

They were afraid. Very afraid.

When the group of men was returning to the village after burying the sorcerer and taking a wash in the canal, they realised that Ali was nowhere to be seen. No one had noticed when he had given them the slip. He had crept up to Amina Chachi's courtyard in the slithering darkness of early dusk, his body still covered in mud, balancing the spade on his left shoulder. It was now or never. His body was aching from last night's fight. The old man never got a chance to teach him the spell, the jinn was surely going to trouble him. If he had learnt the spell he would have used it for something else. When the rain came and moistened the earth, he felt very lonely.

He would have to speak to Amina Chachi about Rabeya today.

Rabeya had spread her locks on the ground like a mass of dark clouds strewn across the sky, and was sitting in the small veranda outside the hut. When she saw Ali she went in. Ali could see the outline of her shoulders and neck in the faint light. The rain lashed him, bringing the smell of the earth. Ali filled his lungs with air and rubbed the rainwater on his face.

Amina Chachi was sitting in the veranda with a rosary in her hand. She opened her eyes with a start and screamed, "Who's there? Who's that in the darkness?"

"It's me, Chachi, Ali."

"Can't you cough or something when you come in? It's dark already, there's no man at home. Is this the way to enter someone's house?"

"Sorry, Chachi, I was lost in thought. I'm feeling quite upset, really. The old man died this morning."

"Has he been buried? Oh, what a day it has been! The poor man, did it have to happen to him of all people? What miracles he had shown us all his life! And when his time came, he couldn't even get a decent burial."

"You're right, Chachi. We dug a grave for him thrice, and each time the earth refused to take him."

Ali had already settled down in the veranda. The desire to listen to a thrilling story was as old as the desire to tell such stories. Bead by bead, the rosary kept moving in Amina Chachi's hand. Ali hunched forward and glanced at the dark and dingy hut. He could hear the rustling of a thick sari. He started telling the story.

When he realised that the two women were almost about to faint, he said, "That's enough for tonight, Chachi, I'll tell you the rest later, or else you'll not be able to sleep."

Fear itself seemed to rush towards the hut in the form of a cold breeze from over the canal.

Ali said, "I've told you earlier too, Chachi, we should think about the marriage now. Why don't I call in the heads of the village and do what's needed? We have enough to live on, thanks to the old man."

Amina Chachi spared no emotions in her expression. "Why should I say no? The girl's grown up now, I'll have to get her married sooner or later."

Her sari rustling, Rabeya left her spot by the door and withdrew into the hut. The silver bangles on her wrist rang out, perhaps in protest. Ali rose to his feet. "I'll leave now. I'll send the formal message tomorrow."

As soon as Ali left, Rameez popped out of the darkness. Amina hadn't realised just when he had stepped into the yard and had been eavesdropping. There was mud all over his body. Without any preamble whatsoever, he walked up to Amina and said, "I warn you, Rabeya's marriage has already been fixed. Ask your daughter if you don't believe me."

Recovering from the initial shock, the woman said, "There's nothing to ask. She's my daughter, I'll get her married to whoever I please."

Rameez growled again, "Don't say I didn't warn you. You remember the sorcerer, don't you? Rabeya will get married to me."

Rameez strode away into the darkness.

Amina said yes to the messenger sent by Ali the next morning. The monsoon was in full swing by now, and seeds were being sown in the fields, and amidst all this, Ali began preparations to bring home a bride. Strangely, Rameez didn't seem to be bothered at all. Instead, he appeared quite busy with land. He said, "A man marries a woman. I shall marry this land of mine. All the women in the world can wait."

The wedding was two or three days away when, as Ali sat chatting with Kobad one evening, Rameez came up and said, "Ali, come with me. We need to build a ridge on the land near the canal. We'll do the eastern side tonight and finish the rest tomorrow."

Rameez had a gamchha wrapped around his face. He seemed taller than he usually did. Kobad nudged Ali in good humour, saying, "This fellow is in seventh heaven right now. Are you sure you want to drag him to the mud in the rain?"

Ali said, "No, that's all right. He and I own the land jointly, we sow together and reap together. I should go."

He picked up a spade and left with his brother.

It must have been around ten at night, though to the villagers it seemed well past midnight. A series of earth-shattering screams from somewhere near the canal pierced the rain and tore through the tragic wails of the wind. The villagers woke up and began to tremble. It seemed to them that the dead sorcerer had risen from his grave, his ghastly cries penetrating the loose earth over his body.

A team of villagers walked towards the canal with lanterns, and saw an extraordinary scene on Rameez's plot of land. The top half of Ali's body, including his head, was buried in the ground.

Someone had dug up the freshly wet and soft earth and buried his head in a hole. The ridge remained untouched.

The villagers were dumbstruck. A horrible sense of terror gripped them. Raham cried in agony, "Ali . . . Ali, my little brother."

At that moment Kobad saw Rameez standing at a distance, staring at the corpse with shock and terror in his eyes. Kobad growled, "Allah, Allah, Ya Rasool Allah!"

Perhaps on hearing Allah's name, the other men gathered their courage and yelled angrily, "Who did this? Who?"

A deep voice was heard behind the crowd. "The sorcerer's jinn."

A cold shiver ran down everyone's spine, but Kobad narrowed his eyes and asked Rameez, "Didn't you call Ali away from his house in the evening?"

An expression of fear and surprise appeared on Rameez's face. He said, "Me? What are you saying? I haven't spoken to him since morning."

"You didn't call him away to build ridges around the land this evening?"

"No, of course not."

"Yes, you did. I was there, sitting with Ali."

Shabir interjected, "How's that possible? Rameez was with me all through the evening at my house. He left for home just a few minutes ago."

A stunned silence descended upon the terrified men. They stood motionless in the rain, glancing at one another.

"Allah, Allah, Ya Rasool!" Kobad roared again. But this time, the men didn't find the courage they needed. Instead, they looked at the land and received another rude shock. There was not a single footprint on the wet ground. It was as if someone had flown down from the sky with Ali's body and shoved his head into the ground.

"The sorcerer's jinn . . . must be the dead man's jinn . . . " A whisper began to rise as they turned around to walk back to the village. No one had the courage to touch Ali's corpse.

But suddenly there was a maddened scream in the dark. They looked around to find Rameez was missing from the group.

Everyone rushed back to the land by the canal to discover a tall young man standing by Ali's body and yelling at the sky above, "Come! Come and fight me, if you dare to! Jinn my foot . . . come!"

It was hard to recognise Rameez from his voice. The villagers had a tough time pulling him away and literally carrying him all the way back to the village. But that very night, they heard a heart-wrenching scream yet again. This time no one dared to investigate. Everyone waited for dawn to break. As the muffled and petrified voices discussed several possibilities, Raham suddenly said, "Where's Rameez? Has anyone seen Rameez?"

Everyone huddled together in sheer terror. Raham alone dashed towards his house in desperation, only to return after some time beating his breast and weeping bitterly, "He's gone. The jinn must have taken him away. It won't rest till it has killed all three of us."

Everyone rushed back to the canal in the morning. Ali's corpse was still buried in the ground, and next to it lay a jet black crow, dead, nailed to the earth by a sharp spear.

Rameez's body was found a couple of yards away. Raham ran up to his brother and turned him around. The villagers yelled, "Is he . . . is he still alive?"

Everyone gathered around Rameez. He was still alive but unconscious.

They carried him back to the village. Rameez opened his eyes after some time. And the villagers heard the strangest of stories from him. Apparently the jinn had come to Rameez around midnight, in the form of his elder brother Raham. It had talked about a plan to bring Ali's corpse back for a proper burial. Rameez had agreed immediately. He had taken the spear along with him. As they approached the spot where Ali was buried, the jinn had turned around and tried to push Rameez to the ground. But Rameez was prepared. He had driven the sword through Raham's chest. He didn't remember anything after that.

Rameez had once again lost his consciousness after narrating the story. It took him one whole month to recover. And then Rabeya came into his home. For the first time in his life, Rameez witnessed a second monsoon in the same year.

THE
AGONY
OF
THE
GHOST

The indigent ghost was sitting on the branch of a neem tree. He was staring at one of the windows of the building with six apartments and wondering whether to enter when the window was slammed shut all of a sudden. The ghost could see part of a kitchen through the glass panes in the upper half of the window. He could also hear the maid of the house clean the plates and pots. The ghost regretted his hesitation—how was he to get in now? He had had a wonderful opportunity to take care of the maid when the window was wide open. All he had had to do was to enter. But the window was shut now, and, contrary to popular belief, ghosts can't walk through walls or closed doors or windows. When he hadn't become a ghost, he used to believe in such stupid stories. But now that he was one, he realised that his primary problem was that he was the past, not the present. He didn't exist now, he had existed at some time in the past. Which essentially meant that there was no place where he could make his presence felt. When he presented himself somewhere, neither he nor anyone else believed in his presence there. Not even once had he imagined when alive that he would have to face such a strange problem after his death. It was true that he could vanish whenever he wished to—the ability to disappear at will was the one true advantage of being a ghost. He never had to try too hard. In fact, it seemed he was always invisible, and that he had to put in a lot of effort to become visible. The poor man would put his hands and feet and head and toes together and try his best to become visible. But much to his horror, everything seemed to float away in a strange manner, and he continued to remain invisible. Jumping up to the rooftop of a five-storied building, or flying from one place to another—he could do all these things. He could even enlarge or shrink his body at will—more or less. But walking through a wall? Or flying in or out through a closed window? He couldn't do those. He had asked around, only to realise that no other ghost could do it either. The advantages of a mortal body were no longer with him, but the disadvantages still remained.

It wasn't as though he had been a ghost forever. He had turned into one quite recently. In fact, he still remembered that fateful night quite clearly. It had been more than a fortnight, but the damned rain was showing no signs of stopping. His wife and the three children were starving, just like him. Dusk fell. The relentless downpour continued in the dark. No lightning or thunder, no growling of the clouds, no breeze—only the steady monotone of the rain falling around his hut. As he lay there listening to the sound, it seemed to him that everyone outside his hut, everyone else in the world, had been long dead, and there was no point of living any more. Because the rains would melt and wash away the earth. All he should do right then was to bring down the knife from the wall and slit the throats of his wife and their little children one by one.

Rainwater was dripping into the hut from holes in the roof. A lonely lantern stood in one corner with soot all over its face, the wick minutes away from going out. Clouds of smoke were billowing out of the vent. A sudden urge overpowered the poor and indigent man, so strong that he couldn't even wait to murder his wife and children. He flung a torn sheet over the beam near the roof of the hut and hanged himself. The tattered sheet ripped into two, but by then the man was dead.

The poor man had felt only one sensation while dying—sharp hunger. He had heard that it didn't hurt any more after death, that there was no pain. Man could rise above hunger and thirst, affliction and agony, burns and bruises. But after he died the poor man realised it was all a cock and bull story. He no longer had a stomach, but he still felt hungry. When he had a belly he could tie a piece of cloth around it to curb his hunger. But he didn't have a belly now. Still, one indisputable advantage of being a ghost was that you were immune to all feelings and emotions except the sensation you had experienced while dying. The poor man had died hungry. So hunger was all he could feel after dying. His wife had died soon after. He bumped into her every now and then. The strong lust he used to feel for her when they were alive was gone now. And she in turn felt nothing but an inconsolable sense of grief for her litter.

Be that as it may, the window to the kitchen had now been shut. Such a huge building, such a large backyard, and not a single open window! What would he do now?

He needed a well-fed and yet frail human right away. Perhaps a woman. One who would roll her eyes and collapse on the floor. Then he could take his time to take all the food in her stomach into his own. The ghost was afraid of all those fat, rich, broad-chested, pot-bellied gentlemen lying on their beds and chewing on their paan. He never even walked past them—neither in life, nor in death.

It was becoming impossible to bear the pangs of hunger any-more. He shook his head hopelessly and took flight, soaring over the three- and four storied houses, his shadowless form flying out of the town and over the village by the river. The sweet sun of the wintry afternoon was shining over it. The poor phantom flew around, his eyes keenly fixed on the ground below. The villagers were all sitting around, hands on their cheeks—some out in the open, some inside their dark and damp huts. He saw a young girl sitting in one corner of a yard, and an older woman, presumably her mother, trying to untangle her unkempt, unoiled hair.

The girl said something, whereupon her mother delivered three well-timed blows on her back. The hungry ghost was search-ing for a plump woman. One who had had a hearty meal, shoved a paan into her mouth, and lain back on her bed for her after-noon siesta. Her husband would be sleeping next to her. Her cheeks, her eyes, her chin—virtually the entire face—would swollen from sleep. Her stomach would still be full. If only the ghost could find such a woman! He would swoop down on her in the twinkling of an eye. But no matter how hard he looked, the ghost couldn't find such a woman. What's more, it would soon be dark. By the looks of the village, it didn't seem like any of the huts had lights. The ghost noticed that all the women out in the open were as thin as reeds. Finally, with no other option left, he dove down on a young girl standing near the well and possessed her. It worked. Making an ungodly sound, the girl gnashed her teeth and collapsed on the ground. The starving ghost did what he had to, scraping up everything in the girl's stomach. He himself didn't have a stomach, but he did have a fiery hunger, which he tried to satiate with whatever he could gather from the girl's belly. And then he stood up.

But he was nowhere near being satiated. Meanwhile, a crowd had gathered around the girl, splashing water on her face. The desperate ghost gasped as he moved on, looking for someone else. No one but ghosts knew how hard they had to work to possess someone. But what else could he do? An aged lady was relieving herself on the slope leading down to the pond. The ghost pounced on her the moment she stood up. The poor woman let out a scream, fell on the ground, and rolled down the slope till she came up against a low ridge. But this time too, there was barely anything in her stomach. Even though he was a ghost, the smell of the woman's dry innards made him feel like retching. Ghosts possessed the wonderful skill of snatching food from human stomachs. But when there wasn't any food in their bellies in the first place, no ghost had the power to create food. After three such failed attempts, the ghost was about to give up the ghost—once again, that is. And then, suddenly, he ran across his own wife. As soon as he saw her, he realised that she had had her fill of food, although she didn't have a stomach herself.

Our ghost pounced upon his wife with a war-cry. Although she was startled at first, she soon realised that this familiar bite had to be her husband's. She offered no resistance whatsoever.

She had no physical sensations now that she had turned into a ghost. So she simply lay there, numb and motionless.

Soon the ghost stood up, spent, tired and still hungry. He cast a piercing look at his wife, only to realise that while a ghost could plunder all the food from a human stomach without the human's knowledge, it was beyond a ghost's capacity to raid the stomach of another ghost. Hanging his head in shame, guilt and sorrow, the hungry ghost flew away and perched himself on the branch of a neem tree.

THE

VULTURE

Some boys were sitting in a circle after dusk chatting, their backs to the old tamarind tree, bare-bodied and using their dirty half-sleeved shirts as seats, their legs extended, chatting away. A soft groan of pain made them turn their heads. The dry branches of the tamarind tree rustled as something flew through the air, swooping over their heads. It was like a lump of blackness against the faintly dark sky. Narrowly missing the boys, it crashed in the courtyard of the abandoned house close by.

Shouting, the boys raced to the courtyard. All they could see in the faint darkness was a small mound of earth and a dead thorny bush. Their leader realised that of all the birds commonly seen in the air, only the vulture swooped down and ran along the ground till it came to a complete stop. So it was he who first noticed the bird at a distance from the spot where it had landed. It was now looking around in a perplexed manner, trying to see in the dark.

The youngest of the boys said in a terrified voice, "What is that?"

Someone else said, "I don't know."

"It's a bird."

"Must be a bird or something."

"Who knows what creatures come out after dark?" He spit on his own chest.

The lump of darkness stood motionless. One could sense it was trying to hide somewhere. Perhaps in the hollow of an ancient banyan tree, or in some deserted hut smelling of faeces, or maybe behind a bush by the riverbank, or a foxhole. Anywhere.

"God knows what creatures come out after dark, you know. Perhaps it wants something. Or worse still, someone. Come, let's go home."

There were cowherds in the gang as well as school students, and also those who went to school and reared cows, or cut grass, or sowed seeds as and when required.

"What a sissy you are! I'm not going home without finding out what it is."

"No, I want to go home."

"Fine, go. Get out of here."

"Who the hell is going home? I dare you to go past the tamarind tree," said the school-going boy. "We need to find out what that thing is."

Almost everyone stayed back. And then the leader stepped forward. Cautiously, one step at a time. He knew it was a large vulture. He moved in close to the bird, close enough to touch it if he wanted to.

"Who knows what creatures come out after dark? Who knows what it's out to get?" The cowherd was still muttering under his breath.

A sudden gust of wind made dozens of dry leaves fall off the branches of a nearby tree. Ripples appeared on the calm water of the pond, followed by tiny waves. Someone dropped something somewhere in the distance, and a nasty metallic sound broke the silence of the evening.

The boy walked all the way up to the thing and realised it was indeed a vulture. Perhaps it had not been able to return home before the sun had set. It was as good as blind now. A strong stench hit the boy's nose. He knew this odour—it came from the waste land outside the village where the corpses of dead animals and birds were left to rot. It seemed the vulture had bathed in the rotting blood and melting flesh of a carcass minutes ago. The signs of its battle with a dog were still visible in the form of a thick rough feather that had almost been ripped out of its wing.

"It must have been fighting all afternoon. It's still gasping for breath."

Poltu stepped forward, with Jamu and Edai right behind him. Followed by everyone else.

Poltu said, "That's a vulture, isn't it?"

"Of course it's a vulture, are you blind?"

Jamu the cowherd said, "Anyone want to take a guess on whether it's a boy or a girl?"

The leader Rafiq said, "You know, you've got the same brain as that of those cows of yours."

The vulture was still sitting quietly. Perhaps this annoying experience was making it uncomfortable. Rafiq said, "Come, let's have some fun. Let's make it dance."

All the boys started shouting, even the one who had wanted to go home but hadn't dared pass the tamarind tree all by himself.

Rafiq stepped forward and grabbed the vulture by its wings. The ugly bird sprang into action immediately. It had no intention of being captured without putting up a fight. Unfurling its dirty, bloody, foul-smelling wings, it scurried along the narrow lane of the village on its claws.

This was how they took their run up before taking flight. Perhaps this bird could take off too, ridding itself of these insufferable young boys, their cruel curiosity, and fatal games. But that was not to be. The vulture could barely see where it was going. Losing its sense of direction in the dark, it rammed into a wall. The posse of vengeful little devils with cruel intentions was close behind.

But the bird had managed to cross the lane, for it wasn't entirely blind. The snakes that usually poked their hoods out of their holes in the walls on both sides of the lane on sweltering summer evenings had now retreated into the safe confines of their homes on sensing the approach of the vulture.

Running past a shrub of jujubes, through the ruins of a dilapidated hut, ignoring the dirty tract of wasteland, the creature continued trying to lift off into the sky, running faster and faster, squinting to see in the dark, trying to escape with its life. But it was helpless and weak. It had no strength left to hit back at its pursuers. Its beak was hooked, its claws were sharp—but it simply didn't have the strength or the eyesight needed to use them.

One of the boys yelled in the dark. He had stepped on the sharp edge of a bone.

"Let him wait here," Rafiq growled. "We're going to catch that damned bird tonight."

"You! Wait here. We're going to catch that damned bird tonight."

"Or you could go home too."

"He can't! He's bleeding. There's blood all over his feet."

The injured boy said, "Let it bleed, I'm not going home. We're going to catch that damned bird tonight." He limped on, trying to break into a run.

A rotten swamp lay ahead. The bird banked left and took off, trying to fly. But it was flapping its wings far too tentatively. Perhaps it was out of breath, too tired to fly. It came crashing down into the foul water, raising tiny waves that broke against the shore without making any sound whatsoever.

It was a grim, ugly creature that clambered out on the other side of the swamp.

Changed. Soaked. Covered in mud.

The boys had run up to this end of the swamp.

The habitation of the village had thinned out in these parts, rising its dark head once in a while. The bird staggered through two huts and entered an open field.

The boys could barely see one other's faces. They were gasping for breath.

"Run all you like. You can't get away tonight."

"No more, Manik, no more . . . "

"This bugger's done."

"I'm going to catch it tonight."

"Yes, me too."

They pushed on, over the dykes and through the field, up and down the mounds, trampling the grass, being pricked and stung by a thousand thorns that only succeeded in strengthening their determination.

Edai asked Rafiq, "What are you going to do when you've caught it?"

"Nothing. I just want to catch it."

"And then?"

"Hmmm."

"What do you mean hmmm? What will you do after that?"

"First let me catch it. I'll think about what to do afterwards."

No one was talking anymore. No one could talk anymore. They ran through the darkness like spectres.

The wind blowing from the south had stopped scraping their skin. The sound of leaves falling in the mango grove had ceased. The foxes were no longer yelping. The crickets weren't chirping. The darkness was not thickening.

They caught up with the bird in the end. They grabbed it, held it, attacked its wings. They could feel the bird breathing heavily, the hollow of its chest moving up and down like the bellows of a blacksmith—they felt it with their own chests—as the bird struggled to set itself free.

Had the vulture felt the boys' excited heartbeats on its own breast too?

"Is this the one? Are you sure this is the same one?"

"This is the one we have been chasing, right?"

"Why, you don't believe this is the one?"

"I don't know, it looks different somehow."

"Do you smell that? That strong smell?"

"What smell? It's a wretched odour!"

The vulture was indeed emitting the foulest of stenches, which seemed to be borne by an oozing fluid of some kind.

Rafiq said, "Come on now, grab it tight. No, don't hold it by its beak, it'll choke to death."

The cowherd stepped forward and said, "I'll hold the bastard! Let me shower some love on my little birdie!"

Jamu on one side and Rafiq on the other forcefully unfurled the vulture's strong and massive wings.

"Look at those wings! Must be eight or nine arm-lengths at least."

The curled down on the wings tried to puff. The intricately arranged feathers were meant to expand one layer at a time and roll out like a carpet. But the bird was drenched in the muddy waters, and its feathers were wet and heavy. So there were gaping holes between the rows of feathers, which looked miserable. The bird threw both its wings up in the air and surrendered itself to its fate.

And then the second round of running began.

"Run now, run. Put your tails between your legs and run!"

The vulture's weakened legs could hardly keep up with the spirited pace set by the boys. But how did that matter? Its legs gradually gave up. The boys were now dragging it through the field.

"Edo, watch out you bastard! You hit its face on the rock. See if it's dead."

"Who the hell cares? Let's drag the carcass if it's dead."

The rest of the boys screamed in delight as they ran after the dying bird. Shouting and singing. Enjoying themselves. What a beautiful game this was! What was the purpose of this game?

Purpose?

"We're going to skin you alive, you hear? You miserable vulture! You smell like corpses. You sit on the carcass of cows and eat their flesh all day. You fight and claw with dogs and foxes. Why do you think we hate you so much?"

Indeed, the boys hated the very sight of the vulture. It seemed to them that their food was the same as the vulture's food, that their dirty clothes were like the dirty feathers on its body, it reminded them of the bloodsucking money-lender back in the village. No wonder they called him a vulture! Nasty, nasty bird. It always seemed to them that a vulture couldn't digest what it ate. The one grey colour in the whole wide world that saddened them the most was the colour of its feathers. When their own hearts wept on seeing the bodies of tiny babies in ditches or under the tamarind tree, almost but not quite alive, why would this filthy bird choose to swoop down on them and tear apart their soft flesh?

Someone said, "I'm hungry."

"Why, haven't you eaten?"

"I had rice and mutton for lunch."

"Yes, me too. I'm hungry too."

"I hate that shirt of yours."

"Yes, it's thick and rough."

"Yes, just like that vulture!"

"Hamid's father is going to kick the bucket in a day or two. Do you know what he did all afternoon today?"

"I know, he's been gasping for breath for several days now—just like this bitch."

Jamu said "Everyone seems to have that breathing sickness these days, every bastard around. No, no, no . . . you think you can get away from me, eh, Aghor Pandit? You damned money-lender, you?"

Everyone laughed at the mention of Aghor Pandit's name.

The boys jumped around in glee and dashed through the field, over the dyke, through the undulating ground and the tall blades of grass, past the berry bushes and the thorn shrubs, through the jagged remnants of sugarcane stalks on the now-empty fields. Like a ball of dirt, devoid of any feelings of pain or joy whatsoever, dazed and dying, the vulture moved on with them. When the boys halted to catch their breath, it paused, showing no sign of protest, making no attempt to escape.

"Look at all those stars!"

"How come there's no light then?"

"There's no moon, see?"

"There's a breeze though."

"Yes, but it's more like a hot wind."

"I don't know about you, but I'm feeling cold."

"That's because you're frightened, stupid."

"How far do you think we've come?"

"I think we're in the middle of the field right now! They call this the slaughter field! And that over there must be the canal."

"Let's go to the canal, we'll dip this bastard in the water."

They could barely see where they were going. The village had disappeared from the horizon. The sky was too large, the darkness too black.

Jamu said, "Have you heard of the things that take place here at night?"

"Please, I beg of you. Let's not talk about those things."

"Late in the night, when everyone's asleep, tamarind trees pop out of the ground, waving their branches to call the villagers. The doors of the huts open on their own, and, be it man or woman, everyone starts walking in their sleep till they wake up suddenly to find themselves in the middle of this field, surrounded by black tamarind trees. They find these trees wherever they look. Who knows what creatures come out after dark?"

The vulture suddenly resembled a black cat. None of the boys dared touch it anymore.

"Isn't it possible that all of us are actually ghosts, and we've simply taken on human form?"

"No, no, Edai, I'm not a ghost, I'm human!"

"Well then touch me and find out for yourself. If I'm not human I'll vanish into thin air as soon as you touch me. Come on, touch me and check for yourself."

"No . . . I can't."

All of them sat down by the side of the canal, maintaining a cautious distance from one another, looking at each other with keen suspicion, pinching themselves. They had let the vulture go. It was lying in a heap.

"Must be past midnight, no?"

"Who knows? It could be just after dusk, or it could be well past midnight."

The boys had lost all sense of time playing the little game of theirs. Someone said, "I heard the fox cry out thrice a short while ago."

"Then it's way past midnight. Dawn will break soon."

"Let's get into the water."

Everyone ran down the slope and waded into the water. A strong breeze blew over the shallow water of the canal, in which the vulture was dipped, drenching it once again.

"Aren't we going to give this bugger anything to eat?"

"What do you think it's going to eat? Do you see any corpses around?"

Jamu said, "Get some straw, let it eat that. Bastard!"

Someone ran out to the field and came back with some long strands of straw.

Rafiq said, "It's not a cow, how can it . . . well, all right . . . it'll have to swallow this for now."

"Yes, yes, make it eat."

"Give me that stick of yours."

"Very good! Yes, pry its beak open like that, yes . . . now hold it this way."

The vulture let out a horrible cackling sound. Two of the boys wrung its neck, one of them pried its beaks open with the stick and the rest started shoving bits and pieces of straw down its throat.

"Swallow it, you bastard. Die, die, you filthy bitch!"

"Hey, hey . . . .watch this . . . see what I do."

Rafiq grabbed a feather on the vulture's body and pulled at it with all his might. Silently, the feather came loose. The vulture shuddered. And then everyone started plucking out its feathers. It looked like a large ugly hen after sometime.

The boys were walking back to the village. Swaying and staggering, limping and tripping, exhausted and famished. They examined their tattered shirts. They talked about the next day's plans. As soon as they entered the village they saw something white under the palm tree.

Jamu said, "No, don't. Let's take the other route."

"But your house is that way, no? Let's go and find out what that is."

"Since my house is that way, I know who those two are."

"Who?"

"Why the hell do you want to know?"

"Tell me."

"The man on the left is Zamiruddi, and that's Kadu Sheikh's whore of a sister."

"What the hell are they doing over there?"

"I don't care. Come on, let's go."

Just before the crack of dawn, when the night is at its darkest, the boys collapsed on their torn mats in their respective homes and fell asleep at once. Spent and starving, the boys let go of all their worries and anxieties and fell asleep. They didn't wake up even after the sun rose and began to shine brightly above the villagers' heads.

The vulture lay dead a yard or so from the palm tree, in full sight of everyone. It had brought up lumps of rotting flesh dying. How big it looked! Pieces of straw were still sticking out of its open mouth. It had turned its naked wings inside out, dropping dead on the dusty ground. One by one, dozens of other vultures began to swoop down and gather around it. But a vulture doesn't eat another vulture's flesh. Right next to the dead vulture was the tiny body of a newborn baby. It was this baby that had attracted the flock. They alighted, screeching in insane, drunken delight.

The dead baby had also succeeded in pulling the residents out of their huts.

"Who did this?"

Men and women watched the vultures closing in on the baby's corpse. Everyone was there. Except Kadu Sheikh's widowed sister. She was sick. In the bright light of the day, she looked as pale as death itself.

THROUGHOUT

· THE

AFTERNOON

Twelve-year-old Kankon stepped out of the house for a stroll, without a smile on his face or shoes on his feet. His mother said, "Where are you going?" So he had to answer, "I'm not going any-where, I'll be right here." Kankon knew ma wouldn't ask too many questions, because the doctor had come, and he had said that grandpa would die today. Or tomorrow. Or maybe day after tomorrow. But he would die for sure. So ma knew that grandpa was dying. Kankon knew it too. Winter had arrived. All the warm clothes had been brought out of the cupboards. So had the quilts, which had been put out in the sun. Grandpa would have trouble dying in the cold. He would probably prefer to die in the warmth of the sun. He would tell ma, "Take me outside, I want to die under the sun."

The leaves looked ugly in winter. It was very cold in the shade, and the earth looked as white as bleached bones beneath the grass. The grass hadn't turned yellow yet, but it would soon. The dew on the dying blades had not dried yet at this time of day. The sun had peeped out just once from behind the clouds. A dove cooed from a date tree, making Kankon restless and sad.

"Everything is dying," Kankon wanted to say aloud, but there was no one nearby to listen. The leaves were dying, the grass was dying, the gardens were all but empty and barren—pale and yellow. They were all dying, for sure! And grandpa was dying with them. Kankon thought it was high time he spoke to them before they died—to the grass, the leaves, the sky. As the cold breeze shook him to his bones, Kankon stepped out of the house without his shirt. He tugged at the hook of his pants with all his might to secure it in place. Rubbing his running nose, he wiped his palm on his bottom. He counted the marbles in his pocket and muttered, "I can't believe they won ten, the bastards!" As the sad memory of his loss returned to him, he stood in the middle of the trail, his head bowed. But he shook the thought off soon. "Grandpa is dying, Kankon, and all you can think of are your stupid marbles?" That's what ma would say, so Kankon made it his own and reprimanded himself with a serious expression on his face and his hands in his pockets.

As he stood there, Kankon wondered why ma wasn't urging him to go to school. But then, why would she? Of course, he wouldn't have to go to school. Today, tomorrow, perhaps the day after tomorrow as well. Because grandpa was dying. He would be dead—either today, or tomorrow, or the next day. In fact, Kankon wouldn't have to go to school until he died. It wasn't right to go to school when someone was dying. People would say all sorts of things. But then, nor was it right to play marbles when someone was dying. It was best to be by the bed of the dying person. Kankon didn't wait a moment longer once this thought crossed his mind. He began walking briskly. The ground beneath his feet felt wet, hard and icily cold. Dead vines and bushes raced past him, dry leaves blowing around in the wind, and whatever little remained of the shiny black water in the ditch all looked at him with grief-stricken eyes as he passed by.

Kankon tripped on the barren road and sliced his toe open. As blood oozed out of the wound, Kankon tried to catch his breath. Grandpa's room was so neat and clean. And so quiet. A chair, a table, windows, doors, the bed, the mattress, the jug of water, grandpa himself—all quiet. And look at our room— Kankon addressed the invisible listener—our room is dirty, I study there, I tear up all kinds of paper, I litter, our room is dirty. The window panes rattle when the wind blows. A filthy room, really filthy. Ma and I sleep in this room. She scolds me when I shout, "Kankon don't shout." Kankon imitated his mother's expression and voice. "Kankon don't shout." Ma is the only quiet one in our room. Everything else is fine.

Of course, Grandpa's room was the best. Right in the middle of the house. Curtains hung on the doors and windows. None of the other rooms had curtains. A neatly arranged creaseless mattress on the bed, a spotless white sheet covered the table. Soft cotton foam on the chair. Bottles of pills on the table, a jug of water, a glass. Not even a dry leaf flying into the room through the window went unnoticed. Ma picked it up with her own hand and tossed it away. The room was dusted thrice a day, and mopped to a mirror-shine. Grandpa had been lying on his back since god knew when. He just couldn't get out of bed, screaming like a lunatic whenever anyone entered. Just like Jatai, the crazy beggar in the market. He bangs his head on his pillow when he got too angry. The old bugger could really scream his lungs out. All he did all day was whine and scream, "I'm hungry, I'm hungry, give me some food." It must be really irritating for ma. Kankon explained to a tree how his grandpa was paralysed and confined to bed. That's why he was always in a foul mood. Not that he could be blamed for it though. He had been dying for a long time now—and yet, somehow, he just wouldn't die. Anyone in his condition would have a foul mood, it wasn't his fault, after all. He must have concluded that, as long as he was alive, he would have to have four meals a day, he would have to shit and piss. But Kankon still made a face at him every now and then.

The old man would be happy when Kankon entered. He would say, "There you are, how are things?"

Kankon might say, "Just came back from school."

"Come, sit by my side."

"I haven't had a wash yet."

"That's all right, come sit."

"No, I have to have my lunch."

"Fine, get out."

Kankon might sit down by his bed then. Grandpa would look around to check that they were alone in the room and then whisper, "What did you have for breakfast today?"

"Rice, hilsa fry, dal, and potato curry," Kankon answered in excitement. "You know grandpa, the curry was delicious!"

"Listen, can you get me a couple of pieces of hilsa fry from the kitchen? Make sure no one sees you?"

"Ma will skin me alive if she catches me."

"She won't find out."

"I can't do it grandpa."

"Please, my boy, I'm starving."

"Why do you do this grandpa? Why do you always ask for things like children do? That's something we do. In any case, I have never thrown tantrums in my life. I eat whatever ma puts on my plate. I never ask for anything more. Didn't you eat this afternoon? Hasn't ma brought you your lunch? Why do you keep asking for food? If you had your way you'd eat a pot of rice and then eat the pot too."

Grandpa wouldn't be listening. "Just two pieces, my boy. I'll give you one."

Kankon would say sternly, "I see. Now you want to bribe me? You've become a miserable old fellow, you know. It's time for you to pop off now." Kankon had learnt the expression from the boys he played with.

The old man would now explode. "That's what you want, I know. That's what all of you want—including that wretched mother of yours. That's why she doesn't give me any food all day."

And then as soon as ma would enter and ask, "What's the matter?" grandpa would immediately break into a smile. "Nothing, we were just talking, that's all!"

"That's all!" Kankon would imitate grandpa.

As he caressed his wounded toe now, Kankon thought, "But now grandpa is dying. Either today, or tomorrow, or day after tomorrow. Doctor Moti has clearly said his time is up. I won't have to go to school till he dies. But . . . I feel sorry for grandpa, really. Too bad he's dying, like the grass, like those vines, like the sky. Everything is dying. Grandpa is a good man, and I feel bad that he's dying. I'd have made him the king had he been alive when I grow up."

Kankon laughed as he remembered the other day when grandpa had called him secretly and said, "Kankon, don't you go to the market these days?"

"Why grandpa?"

"Don't they sell those small geese anymore? Can you get me one?" And then grandpa had become strangely drowsy.

All that grandpa wanted was a small goose, a baalihash. How pretty they looked while flying! Kankon looked up at the sky. It looked pale and ugly. Kankon didn't like it at all. The geese came flying. God knows where they came from. If only he could fly like them! That would have been fun. Some days were so horrible and tedious—grandpa would sleep throughout, ma wouldn't say a word. Kankon felt like running away. Or dying. Kankon tried to remember the day when, for the first time, he had felt like dying. Nayja had lost fifteen marbles that day, so naturally he was furious. "Wipe that stupid smile off your face, do you know where you father is?"

Kankon had said what ma had told him. "He's in Dhaka."

"Is that so? Dhaka? Then why doesn't he come home?"

Holding his head high, Kankon said, "He will."

"He's never coming back, do you know why?"

"Why?"

"Because people will beat the hell out of him."

Kankon yelled, "Why?"

"Your father's run away with a whore."

"What's a whore?"

"You don't know what a whore is? Shame on you, really, shame on you—he doesn't know what a whore is, do you hear?"

The other boys joined Nayja and surrounded Kankon, pinching and poking him, pulling at his hair, making faces and laughing, "He doesn't know what a whore is . . . ho ho ho!"

Kankon had come home in the evening after a fistfight with them and looked for ma. She was busy in the kitchen. Without taking a wash, Kankon opened a book and tried to study. He could hardly concentrate. The book remained open, Kankon kept staring at the darkest corner of the room. And then he began to doze off. He refused to go when ma called him to dinner. Later, when she had cleaned up in the kitchen and come to the room, Kankon asked her, "Ma, where is Abba?"

"In Dhaka."

"Why doesn't he come visit us?"

"He will. Off to bed now. Why didn't you eat?"

"Has abba gone away with a whore?"

Ma stopped what she was doing. Her face turned grave. "Who told you that?"

"Those boys."

Ma said without any hesitation, "They're right."

"What's a whore, Ma?"

With a sharp slap on his face, Ma exploded. "You wretched brat, you want to know what a whore is? I am a whore."

Grandpa's voice was heard from the next room. "What's the matter?"

Fuming with rage, Ma walked up to the other room, pushed the door open angrily and yelled, "Shut up, shut up, I don't want to hear a single word from you. Slimy old bugger. As if you don't know anything!"

"Oh. Yes, all right." Grandpa didn't say another word. Had he dozed off? Or was he still awake? God alone knew. Ma walked back into the bedroom, slammed the door shut, switched off the light and came to bed. There in that dark room, for the first time in his life, Kankon had felt like dying. A whore must be a very bad word. What exactly did it look like, this thing? Kankon wondered, and felt like dying.

That was the first time. And then there was another day when he had felt like dying. Just a few weeks ago. Kankon had come home from school early. It was rather hot. The sun was blazing. The plants were burning. The earth was sizzling. Kankon could hear the crackling sound as the leaves and grass burnt. He could smell it too. That afternoon everything seemed to be dozing in exhaustion. Kankon could visualise their house in the distance, a slithery outline, searing in the heat. Only grandpa's room was cool, a sweet smell of medicine wafting in the air, a jug of water on the table, a glass next to it. The room was in the shade. Grandpa was sleeping. Kankon felt like going into grandpa's room. Grandpa was sleeping, his lips were parted. A crow was sitting in the yard near the mechanical tubewell. It was playing with a small bone. Flying away for a few moments, it returned with a dead rat in its beak, and perched on a plant in the kitchen garden. A grasshopper leapt and disappeared within the grass.

Kankon entered his room and found a fair-skinned man lying on the bed, his head resting in ma's lap. She was running her fingers lightly through the man's hair, and then she brought her face down over his. Kankon turned around, because the crow had started cawing.

"Come," ma said, looking at Kankon with a sad expression in her eyes.

The man rose from the bed, ran his palm over his hair and yawned. Ma said, "This is my son, Kankon."

"I see." The man tapped Kankon lightly on his chin, turned towards ma and said, "I have to go now." Then he walked out into the scorching heat. The smell of burning grass was now inside the room, the crackling sound was in Kankon's ears. The crow was nowhere to be seen. A new little green bird had taken its place on the kitchen plant. A pile of used utensils had been dumped near the tubewell. Ma glanced at it and said, "Kankon, don't tell anyone."

"Who was that man?"

"You will not say anything to anyone."

Kankon was so angry he could barely see. Ma's face was turned towards the yard.

"Yes I will."

"No you won't."

"I will, I'll tell everyone."

"Kankon!"

"Yes, I will tell everyone." It was no longer his rage, but his tears that were now blinding him. "I'll tell anyone and everyone

I wish to." He threw himself on the floor like a chicken whose throat had been casually slit, then jumped up, prancing and repeating, "I'll tell everyone, everyone."

Ma watched him in silence. And as the rays of the sun gradually disappeared, Kankon fell asleep. A congregation of crows that had gathered in the yard began cawing in a chorus. Night had fallen by the time Kankon woke up. Rubbing his eyes, he said to himself, "Kankon, it's time for you to die now." Why had he feel like dying on seeing the man with ma? Was he a bad man? Kankon had seen him once or twice earlier as well, on the main road, driving a shiny motorbike. He had even come to meet grandpa once. Was he a very bad man? Kankon didn't know. What he did know was that if he saw the man on the bed with ma again, either he or his mother should die.

A marble slipped out of Kankon's pocket as he thought about that day while staring at his wound. He stood up with a start and with a heavy heart. He stared at the marble as it rolled away, and remembered what ma had said that morning, "Kankon, I want you to stay at home this evening."

"Why?"

"Don't go out in the afternoon."

Kankon realised ma was talking about grandpa. So he said, "I heard everything the doctor told you."

"Did you? Don't go out, and . . . " ma's voice trembled a little. Kankon looked up at her. "Your abba will come this evening."

"Really? When?"

"I told you, this evening."

"That'll be fun!"

"Stay at home." Ma didn't say anything more.

But as he remembered what Ma had said that morning, Kankon felt quite sad. Fun? What fun? That man, that fair-skinned man—he no longer came. Sometimes, when he was lost in his school books, Kankon suddenly felt as though the man had stepped into the room and was standing behind him. As though he had always been in the room, with his head in ma's lap. It had been a long time since Kankon had sat in ma's lap. This was quite natural, for he had grown up. Do you sit in your mother's lap when you've grown up? Of course not. But why did ma never pull him into her lap? He might not let her, but she never even tried. Why? In which room would abba sleep? And that whore word—Kankon had learnt the meaning—what a filthy word it was! But ma had said it was true. So then, being her son, he shouldn't want to meet abba, should he? Kankon shook his hair out of his eyes with a flick of his head.

Suddenly there was a strange sound overhead. Kankon shaded his eyes from the sun and looked up at the sky. A large flock of geese were flying by, their feet tucked back, their necks thrust forward. The sun was shining on their black wings, while their snuff-coloured throat had a golden tinge. The flock suddenly banked towards the lake, forming a V.

Forgetting all his pain and hurt, Kankon clapped his hands and said, "Where were you all these days? Why don't you fly down to me? There's nothing to fear. I know grandpa wanted to eat one of you. But grandpa will die soon—either today, or tomorrow, or day after tomorrow. You don't have to worry about him. Come, be my friend."

Paying no heed to his invitation, the geese cut through the air and flew towards the lake. Kankon picked up his marble, put it in his pocket, and took a piss in the grass. Then he rubbed his running nose and wiped his palm on his bottom. And then he gave chase.

Kankon ran through the dry fields, through land full of weeds, through the chest-high bushy outgrowth, through the dense jungle. A small dove sitting in the abandoned courtyard of the dilapidated mansion noticed Kankon rushing through the ruins and took flight. A fox was resting with her eyes shut. Dashing through the dense foliage, Kankon nearly tripped over her. The fox stepped aside, looking intensely irritated. Kankon watched it for sometime in a daze. Then he started running again.

He couldn't see the geese anymore. Even the sunlight was dying. Kankon saw the train tracks in front of him. The field was spread out in the distance, and the huge lake was on the other side of the tracks. It was so large that it frightened Kankon. Where had the geese gone? Kankon felt exhausted having run such a great distance without pausing for breath, and sat down on the narrow ridge below the tracks. He looked around, but he had no way of knowing which direction his house lay in. And the geese—Kankon's heart filled with grief on losing sight of them. If only he could die now. Perhaps he would be able to rise above the ground and fly in the sky. Maybe he would be able to spot the geese and fly with them. But the truth was that, instead of him, it was grandpa who was dying. Perhaps he was dead by now. And then he thought of ma, and a strong surge of emotion swelled in his throat. Wasn't ma dead too? Yes, she was dead. Would he be able to face abba this evening? Would the other woman be with him?

The desire to die had become very intense by now—Kankon had never wanted to die so badly. The grass, the leaves, the sky, the sunshine, everything around him wanted to die along with him.

And at that very moment, the flock of geese rose into the sky once more, so that Kankon could see them again. He climbed the slope towards the railway tracks with his eyes fixed on the birds. There they were, taking flight! He looked around with a smile. The sun had almost set, but the tracks were shining brightly.

The three o'clock express rushed over them with a thunderous sound and in cruel, unforgiving glee, like a monster. And then it was all quiet . . . silent . . . serene.